Mommy's Pretty Girl

Mommy makes everything better. That's what Meg learned as she entered an MDLG relationship with Anna who made all her ABDL dreams come true

By Tina Moore

Table of Contents

Chapter 1

Anna hated the flight back home. The busy crowds, the airport security, the way she always seemed to set the body scanners off made her cringe even thinking about it. Anna was the CEO of a successful lighting franchise specializing in high-end lighting fixtures. As part of her job, she would routinely travel abroad to inspect the manufacturing processes, explore different materials, and generally make sure everything was running smoothly. But over the 15years of being the CEO, Anna had increasingly developed a strong disliking to the travel side of her job. After going through a divorce, watching her parents pass on, and her dog getting on in years, Anna wanted to trade her high-flying career, for something a little more grounding. She would often fantasize about sitting in a bay window of a cozy white cottage, overlooking a garden filled with colorful flowers.

The next part of her fantasy always thrilled her. The thought that a young, sweet girl would be there, needing her, craving her attention. She only let herself think of the things she would do to the girl, how she would control her with such loving care, late at night when she would slide her hand between her thighs, and imagine it was the girl's hand touching her and not her own.

A smirk came over Anna's face as she looked around the waiting gate, watching at a group of girls in their mid 20's. Anna always loved how these types of young, vibrant, and boisterous girls never seemed to dress for the weather or the occasion. This group was one of the same. In the middle of winter, not one of them had a coat which would keep the cold out, their short skirts showed the bare skin of their long toned legs, their backpacks slung over one shoulder, and the jackets that they did have were open, showing off tight t-shirts with trendy logos. One, in particular, caught Anna's attention. The quiet one at the back of the group, talking on her phone and looking

Elogio per i misteri di Janie Juke

'Fu una grande trovata. Una bibliotecaria che si trasforma in investigatrice nell'Inghilterra del 1960. Janie Juke, un'appassionata di Agatha Christie, è un'amabile protagonista. Un vero svoltar pagina. Ho comprato il prossimo libro della serie… Sperando che ce ne saranno molti altri in arrivo.'

'Sono entrato direttamente nella storia… mi piace molto il modo in cui l'autore ha dipinto gli anni 60'… mi sentivo come se fossi lì.'

'Intrigante storia poliziesca con ambientazioni incantevoli e personaggi interessanti. Non vedo l'ora di vedere cosa risolverà la prossima volta Janie Juke.'

'Ho amato ogni pagina e non riuscivo ad interrompermi. Non riesco ad aspettare sino al prossimo della serie.'

'Libro completamente piacevole. Mi ha tenuta interessata sino alla fine. Attendo con ansia il prossimo.'

'Gli scorci sulla Seconda Guerra Mondiale sono particolarmente buoni. La scrittura solida, grande storia, e Janie come personaggio sta crescendo dentro di me. Spero ce ne saranno altri in questa serie.'

Riguardo l'autore

Isabella ha riscoperto l'amore per la scrittura durante due anni felici trascorsi lavorando e completando il suo Master in Scrittura Professionale.

L'ambientazione per la serie dei misteri di **Janie Juke** è quella dell'area dove Isabella è nata e ha vissuto gran parte della sua vita. Quando descrive Tamarisk Bay descrive la sua città natale St Leonards-on-Sea, nell'East Sussex ed i suoi dintorni.

A parte il suo amore per la scrittura, Isabel ha una vera passione per tutti i tipi di caravan. Ha trascorso diversi anni viaggiando nel Regno Unito e all'estero e negli ultimi tempi sta gestendo un piccolo campeggio nel West Sussex, insieme al marito.

Il suo fedele compagno, Hamish, un terrier scozzese, è sempre accanto a lei.

Scopri di più su Isabella, i suoi libri pubblicati, così come i prossimi titoli su: **www.isabellamuir.com** e segui Isabella su Twitter: **@SussexMysteries**

Dello stesso autore

LA BORSA RICAMATA
OGGETTI SMARRITI

rather distressed. She was dressed slightly different to the others, with her fluffy baby pink sweater matching her style-faded black skirt, her black combat boots with the laces undone, and her gray backpack made Anna instantly wet. Anna shifted in her seat, rubbing her thighs together discreetly, smiling at herself as she felt her clit beginning to throb.

Oh, the things I would do to you, Anna thought to herself as the girl bent down to put something into her backpack before standing back up and flicking her hair almost in slow motion. The light, catching her blonde hair as she began to walk quickly, trying to catch up with her friends who were now sitting at the café across from the waiting gate. Anna checked her watch, seeing that it was ten minutes to boarding and decided she wanted closer proximity to the blonde, so getting up, she put her expensive, designer handbag on her arm and sauntered over to the café. Anna was amused at the looks she got, wondering if the people looking at her were thinking the same thoughts she was thinking about the blonde. Although nearing 46 years old, Anna had maintained an active lifestyle. What was more was that she had never been short of looking after herself, and her polished and refined body complimented her flawless and sophisticated style. After living in France for several years, Anna had learned that style is quite different from fashion. As Anna crossed the corridor and walked into the café, she flicked her wavy chocolate brown locks and began to take off her long, deep emerald green coat and drape it over her arm. Anna's eyes searched for the girl, delighting in the sight of the blonde sitting in the corner of the café. She was still busy on her phone as her friends talked around her. No, not talking, they were in the midst of a conversation which had deemed that shouting was the more appropriate form of communication. This time, she was messaging feverously, and as Anna ordered a coffee, she knew just how she would get the blonde's attention.

"Any sugar, Ma'am?" The boy behind the

counter asked, making Anna smile.

"No thanks," Anna replied, amused that the boy blushed before looking away. Anna's dark pink satin blouse gaped just enough to expose her ample cleavage, and she imagined the boy jerking himself off to her image the moment he got home. She took her coffee, turned around, and rechecked her watch, enjoying how the diamonds within it glistened under the lights.

"Excuse me," Anna said, walking over to the group of girls, and waiting for them to go quiet and give her their attention. She liked the looks they gave her, unsure if she was about to tell them to be quiet or if she was just a sweet, mature lady needing something else. The tension, extended by Anna smiling at them as though she didn't want to rip their clothes off right there and then.

"May I trouble you for the sugar?" Anna asked, watching as they relaxed and laughed before trying to reach for the sugar, only to be beaten in holding it.

"Here," the blonde said, Anna, trying to

keep her eyes from undressing the girl as she held out the sugar to Anna without looking up from her phone.

"Thank you," Anna said, deliberately touching the girl's hand as she took the jar, causing the girl to look up at her, double-taking and beginning to blush. Anna smiled at her knowingly, before taking the jar and walking back to where her handbag was claiming an entire table.

"Dude, you are so red!" Anna heard one of the girl's tease, making the others laugh along.

"What?! She's hot!" Anna heard the blonde say, enjoying the moments she had just stolen and sighed in content as she sipped her coffee and waited for her seat number to be called over the speaker.

Chapter 2

"Now boarding seats M-R," the announcer called over the system. Anna stood up and made her way out of the café. Much to her delight, she heard the sounds of the girl's laughter and general joyfulness behind her. Passing the attendant her ticket, Anna passed through the tunnel and moved down the ramp. She sighed, wishing that she had booked the upgrade when she had the chance. The thought of being stuck sitting next to somebody suddenly made Anna more agitated than she had first thought it would. With the company policy deeming that she could have the upgrade or keep the money on the business account for essential situations like dinners and an additional spending allowance. This trip Anna had decided to use the extra money on a shopping trip, but as the plane began to fill, she could think of nothing better than sipping champagne in her quiet pod.

"Hey," Anna heard, turning her head back toward the aisle to see the blonde standing in front of her.

"Hello," Anna replied, trying not to look as excited as she felt. The blonde reached up, putting her backpack in the overhead locker, her sweater riding up, and Anna seeing her exposed tummy, the faint lines of her abs making Anna want to reach out and touch her. Waiting to see that the girl had put her things away, Anna got up from her seat and made room for the girl to sit in her allocated spot by the window.

"I'm Meg," the blonde said, making Anna smirk.

"Sweet name. I'm Anna," Anna replied, seeing Meg nod her head before putting her headphones on and looking out the window. Anna sat back in her seat, delighted that she didn't book the upgrade and hoping that the last seat in their row would remain empty. With one seat between herself and Meg, Anna knew that there was plenty of space to relax and enjoy the flight, even if most of the flight would be in darkness. Anna always took the night flight because she didn't want to waste the day time traveling.

The air hostess ran through the safety procedures. Anna was amused the Meg didn't feel the need to listen to them and continued to stare out the window. The plane jerked forward, and Anna knew that she had 13 hours to get what she wanted, which was Meg's unwavering desire to be Anna's baby girl.

They spent the first hour in silence. Anna spent her time flicking through her magazine and Meg with her headphones on. Dinner came and went, Meg hardly touching her food and Anna taking out the snacks that she had bought, uninspired by the selection of airplane dinners on offer. It wasn't until the lights went out that Meg took her headphones off and began to look around for the inflight blanket.

"Damn," Meg softly said, assuming that Anna was asleep. Anna turned her body to face

Meg, who looked at her apologetically.

"Sorry, I didn't mean to wake you," Meg said, Anna, reaching out to touch her forearm.

"You didn't wake me, sweetie. What is it?" Anna asked, Meg's head tilt and wide eyes making her smile.

"Um, I can't find my blanket," Meg said, shaking off the feeling the older woman was giving her. Anna took her hand off the girl and began to help her look.

"I think they only gave us one," Anna said, looking back to see if there was a hostess readily available. Turning back to Meg when there was no one in sight, Anna took her blanket off and draped it over the girl.

"Here, have mine, I'll get a new one," Anna said, placing her hand on the girl's cheek affectionately when Meg began to protest, quieting her immediately.

"I insist," Anna said, getting up and walking down the aisle. Meg smiled to herself and wrapped the blanket around her body, enjoying how Anna's body had made it warm. Meg closed her eyes and sighed as the smell of Anna's perfume soothed her, making her want the older woman's affection even more.

My god she smells good, Meg thought to herself, placing one arm underneath the blanket and tentatively stroking herself between her thighs for just long enough to take the edge off before Anna reappeared.

"Did you get one," Meg said, watching as Anna unwrapped not one but two new blankets.

"I got two. I thought maybe we might need an extra one. Who knows," Anna replied, smirking at Meg.

"Cool," Meg replied as Anna sat back down, watching as Meg stirred, trying to find a comfortable spot.

"Maybe we should put these armrests up?" Anna suggested, Meg nodding her head in agreeance.

"And take it in turns stretching out," Meg added, Anna, thinking for a moment.

"Good idea," Anna said, kicking off her heels and undoing another one of her blouse buttons.

"You go first," Anna said, enjoying how Meg watched her.

"Ok. Thanks," Meg slowly replied as her eyes lingered on Anna's full breasts, which were now on display. She curled herself up into the fetal position and took up the space of her seat and the middle seat, which had luckily never remained empty. Anna looked down at the girl's shivering body and placed the spare blanket over the top of her, causing Meg to look up.

"Thanks," Meg softly said before smiling at Anna and turning her head back to try and fall asleep. Anna knew that she would get no rest as the girl's head slightly touched her thigh, more so when Meg had fallen asleep. Anna smiled to herself.

If this is the closest thing I get to her touching me, it will do, Anna thought to herself, looking down at the beautifully innocent girl resting against her thigh. She felt her nipples harden, her pussy moisten and knew that she was dropping into Mommy space. Yet it was when Meg stirred, whined softly in her sleep, and placed her head in Anna's lap that Anna knew that this baby girl needed her.

What a sweet little kitten, Anna thought to herself as she tossed up whether or not to begin to stroke the girl's hair. Deciding against it, Anna let the girl continue to sleep, her thumb coming up and starting to be sucked, driving Anna almost over the edge.

Oh, what the fuck, Anna thought in agony as she watched Meg. Anna lifted herself off the seat slightly, waking Meg up and making her sit up, startled that she had entered her little space in her sleep.

"Oh my god, I am so sorry, I," Meg began to say, getting up off of Anna.

"Shh, it's ok, come on," Anna cooed, as she pushed Meg back down onto her lap, and started to stroke her hair.

"Is it ok if I do this, sweetie?" Anna asked

Meg, nodding her head but keeping her body rigid, embarrassed, and unsure how to feel.

"It's totally fine honey, I don't mind at all," Anna said, smiling as she felt Meg's body begin to relax. Anna reached down and took Meg's hand in hers, bringing her thumb back up to her mouth, Meg parting her lips and starting to suck her thumb again.

"There you go," Anna cooed as she felt Meg fully relax as she closed her eyes and fell back asleep.

What a precious little girl, Anna thought as she stroked Meg's soft blonde hair.

A perfect little baby, she added, sweeping the baby hairs out of Meg's face.

Chapter 3

Meg slept for the better part of three hours, tossing and turning and melting Anna's heart.

Oh my, Anna thought as Meg rolled onto her other side, pressing her face close against Anna's stomach. Anna let her left arm sit on the side of Meg's ass, petting her gently as she slept, her other hand holding Meg's head in place, not wanting it to roll back and off her lap.

If only you were mine, Anna thought, imagining putting Meg in all sorts of cute outfits, giving her baths, and having cuddle time be a nightly occurrence. Just as she was thinking how sweet Meg's pink sweater was, Meg blinked her eyes open.

"Hey," Meg said, taking her thumb out of her mouth and rubbing her eyes but continuing to lay in Anna's lap.

"Hi honey," Anna replied, stroking Meg's

cheek with her thumb and smiling as Meg suddenly opened her arms and wrapped them around Anna's waist.

"Thanks for letting me cuddle," Meg said, Anna, only just making out the words as Meg buried her face in the older woman's lap.

"It's my pleasure. But it's the middle of the night now, you need to go back to sleep, or you'll have a hard time in the morning," Anna said, making Meg laugh.

"I'm going to have a hard time regardless," Meg said, the annoyance in her voice evident.

"Oh? Why is that?" Anna asked, wanting to know more. Meg sat up, much to Anna's disappointment, but she watched as the girl took out her phone. Meg flicked through the photos, stopping when she found the one she wanted.

"This is my boyfriend, was my boyfriend. And this used to be my best friend. They have been sleeping together, and I just found out," Meg explained, her face full of anger and hurt.

"That's awful, I am so sorry," Anna said,

reaching out and wrapping her arm around Meg. Meg just snuggled in, happily surprised that the hot older woman was so affectionate.

"Yeah, and what is worse is that I found out while I was away, and when I confronted him about it, he got so mad and threw all my stuff out onto the curb. Who knows what is left there by the time I get back home," Meg said, burying her face into the side of Anna's generous breast. Anna held her, not saying a word, but comforting Meg all the same.

"He sounds like a real piece of work," Anna said when she finally spoke.

"Yeah," Meg replied, sniffling and wiping her tears away.

"In hindsight, I probably should have kept quiet about it until I got all my stuff out, but I was just so mad," Meg thoughtfully said, thinking out loud.

"Well, you're young, you learn those things with experience and over time," Anna said, thinking back to her messy divorce, before smiling down at Meg.

"I bet you've never been in such a fucked up situation," Meg said, feeling sorry for herself.

"Language, young lady," Anna said, enjoying the small laugh she elicited from Meg as she raised an eyebrow at her.

"And yes, I have. Lucky for me, we were already married, and he was rich. So I got half his shit, and the day it was finally all over, I was able to start living the life I had always wanted to live," Anna said, remembering how it had felt going into a lesbian bar for the first time.

"What sort of life was that?" Meg asked, wondering how she was meant to rebuild her own life.

"Well, for one, I never really liked men. So I explored being with a woman, and I discovered how much I like younger women. I bought an apartment in the middle of the arts district and go to all manner of art events. It felt like I was breathing for the first time," Anna replied, getting lost in the feeling of freedom before looking back down as Meg looked wide-eyed up at her.

"It sounds nice. I guess I can start over now. Maybe the bastard, I mean, asshole, argh shit, the mean man did me a favor," Meg said, trying to stop herself from swearing but struggling to think of an alternative. Anna felt herself swell on the inside as she watched Meg try and please her.

"Good girl. Little ladies like you don't need to use such foul language," Anna said, involuntarily kissing Meg's forehead.

"Sorry, I. You are just so sweet," Anna said, blushing as she thought she overstepped.

"It's cool. I like it. I like girls too," Meg said, making Anna laugh.

"It's been a long time since I've been called a girl," she replied, making Meg bite her bottom lip.

"I just meant," Meg began to say, stopping when Anna placed a finger over Meg's lips.

"I know what you meant, sweetheart," Anna said, closing her eyes and putting her head back.

"You can rest on me if you want, it's only

fair after I pretty much just crashed on top of you without any warning," Meg said, seeing that Anna was tired. Anna smiled, keeping her eyes closed until she turned her head to look at Meg, opening her eyes slowly, happy that her gesture gave her the desired result, seeing Meg's eyes reflect her lustful gaze.

"It's ok, honey. I am very comfortable. Come here," Anna said, patting her lap, delighted at how Meg obediently lay back down, relaxing on Anna's lap as Anna stroked her back to sleep. Anna closed her eyes, feeling the girl's fluffy sweater under her fingertips as she too relaxed and fell asleep.

"Would you like some snacks?" Anna heard the air hostess ask as she made her way down the aisle. Anna looked at the screen in front of her, seeing that the plane was only a few hours off, landing back home.

"Yes, thank you," Anna said when the air hostess offered her the packet of chips, nuts, and a drink.

"Oh, wait a moment, I need some for, baby girl here," Anna said, referring to Meg laying on her lap. Unbeknownst to Anna, Meg had been awake for over an hour, and as Anna collected snacks for Meg, Meg smiled, feeling taken care of for the first time in a long time.

"Sorry, Ma'am, of course," the air hostess said apologetically, giving Anna extra as she recognized her from all the times she had been in first class.

"It's not like you to be sitting back here. Would you like me to move you to first-class?" The air hostess said, making Anna smile.

"No, it's fine, darling, but thank you. I am more than happy here," Anna said, patting Meg affectionately. The air hostess smiled and nodded her head and continued to walk down the aisle.

"You didn't have to turn down first class just to sit here with me!" Meg exclaimed, sitting up and looking at Anna like she had lost her mind.

"Oh, hello there, little miss eavesdropper," Anna teased, making Meg laugh.

"I go, first-class, all the time. It doesn't have anything on this," Anna added, making Meg shake her head.

"Thanks for getting me snacks," Meg said, picking up a packet of chips, realizing how hungry she had become while sleeping.

"My pleasure," Anna said, taking down the tray and placing the rest on top.

"So, where's home for you?" Anna asked, opening up a can of soda.

"Well, it was on the south side out of town. But who knows now. I guess I'll just crash at my friends' house until I figure out what the, what on earth I'm going to do," Meg said, smiling at herself for not swearing.

"I see. Well, here, take my number, and if you need anything, I want you to call me," Anna said, taking out her business card and handing it to Meg.

"Thanks, but I'll be ok," Meg said, taking the card and putting it in her skirt pocket.

"And I'm sure you will be, but just in case,"

Anna said, admiring the girl's slim legs. The seatbelt sign flashed on, and the captain called for the cabin crew to prepare for landing. Anna smiled at Meg as she took her place back by the window, put on her headphones, and looked out onto the city below as the morning sun greeted them.

"Well, bye," Meg said, reaching out to grab Anna's wrist as the headed out of the tunnel and into the airport. Anna looked down to see Meg's hand and smiled.

"Goodbye," Anna said, her eyes dancing with desire as she tore herself away from Meg, winking at her as she turned her head and began to walk away.

"What was that about?" One of Meg's friends said, coming over to her. Meg continued to watch Anna leave, wanting to run after her, but not knowing what she should say when she reached her.

"I don't know, nothing, I guess," Meg said, shrugging her shoulders and turning to walk in the opposite direction.

Anna collected her bags, headed out to the car waiting for her, closed the door, and sighed as the car drove away. She closed her eyes, thought back to how divine it had felt to hold onto Meg, how her hair was warm and soft, and how sweet she looked sucking her thumb as she slept. Anna sighed once more, opening her eyes and shaking her head.

Well, that was lovely, she thought to herself, reaching for the bottle of chilled sparkling water and pouring herself a glass. She was headed home, but not before she ate breakfast at one of her favorite cafes. The financial freedom is what she loved about the job, the seemingly unlimited funds to enjoy life at the level she so desired.

The car pulled into the street, stopped at the entrance at the café. The driver passed the keys to the valet, and both Anna and her driver walked inside. After flight café mornings had become somewhat of a tradition for the two, who never spoke to each other, but enjoyed their dynamic nonetheless.

"I'll take the scrambled eggs and sausages and a black coffee," the driver said to the waitress.

"And for me, I will have the Bircher muesli with fruits, and a green juice," Anna said, handing the waitress the menus back. They looked out the window and out onto the elegant street. Anna thought back to how she used to walk up this street years ago, wondering what it would be like to be one of the people in one of these cafes, looking out and daydreaming about how perfect their lives were.

Is it everything I had hoped for? Anna thought to herself as she sipped her juice.

A few things are missing, she added, as she saw a couple holding hands and walking down the street. She thought back to how she had thrown caution to the wind in her younger days. The way she was always sweeping up those around her. In the hurricane, that was her life, somewhere between then and now, she had settled down and become grounded. Anna laughed to herself as she remembered the way she would dance and skip along with her friends as they walked down the street. Seeing that group of girls with Meg last night had reminded her of how she must have looked to strangers, and it made her smile as she fondly thought of all her youthful memories.

"Oh, to be 20 again," Anna said out loud, her driver smiling to himself and shaking his head. Anna liked that he never felt the need to engage her in conversation. When she was picking a drive that was one of the requirements, that they mustn't want to get to know her or talk to her for that matter, she appreciated that he kept his silence.

As they finished their breakfast, Anna paid on the business card, and they headed out the door to continue their drive. Anna took her place in the back seat, reaching into her phone, disappointed that Meg hadn't called.

She probably won't. You really shouldn't get your hopes up, Anna thought to herself as they veered out onto the road. Anna never had trouble getting a girl to lust over her, that was evident by the way she had so easily made contact with Meg, yet it was what came after that always seemed to ruin everything. Anna would want the girl's attention, her affection, and to be in a relationship far quicker than the girl was ready for, which then in turn always made the girl run away from her.

Chapter 4

Meg shared a taxi with her friends to the apartment where she and her ex used to live.

"Thanks, guys, this was an enjoyable trip. Sorry about the last bit," she said, paying her share and getting out of the taxi. She saw what was left of her stuff on the sidewalk and collected it in her arms. Her friends jumped out of the cab, offering for her to stay with one of them, but she declined. It was bad enough that she had to share the taxi with her backstabbing ex-best friend, she didn't want that bitch to know where she was going to stay.

"Do you want to come in? Here, have the key," Meg said to her as she looked into the taxi before throwing the key at her ex best-friend. Meg didn't wait to see what the response was as she took off up the street, only stopping when she was around the corner. Crying, Meg sat in the gutter and felt more lost than she had ever felt in her life.

Ok, I've got a couple of hundred dollars, my laptop, phone, everything that I took on my trip and this stuff here, Meg thought to herself, trying to calm herself down. She looked up at the gray sky and begged for it not to rain as she opened up her suitcase and put her stuff from the sidewalk in before closing it back up. Meg thought about the nice lady on the plane and tossed up the idea of ringing her.

She will think I'm so weird, Meg thought, taking the card out just to put it back into her pocket.

Fuck it, Meg thought, quickly taking it out again and ringing the number.

"Hello?" Anna said down the phone, Meg smiling as she heard the woman's familiar voice.

"Hi, um, it's Meg, the girl you were sitting next to on the plane?" Meg said, hoping that Anna would remember her.

"Meg, how are you? Lovely to hear from you," Anna said, making Meg smile.

"Um, so you know how you said if I needed anything, I should call you? Well, you wouldn't happen to be cool with me staying with you for a few days, would you?" Meg said, scrunching her face up as she heard how pathetic she sounded. Hearing Anna laugh down the phone was also not helping.

"Of course, I would be cool with you staying. I have a guest room set up, ready to go. Would you like to give me you the address, and I can pick you up, or do you want to make your way here?" Anna asked, snapping her fingers at her driver just as he was about to get back into the car after dropping her off.

"I can make my way there. What's the address?" Meg said. Anna looked up at the driver, smiled, and waved him off before texting Meg the address.

"I will see you soon," Anna said, both surprised and delighted at how her day was unfolding.

After receiving the address, Meg started punched in the details into her phone and began to follow the directions to get to Anna's house. She decided the most cost-effective way would be to take the two trains across town, knowing that getting stuck in midmorning traffic would make for a hefty fare. She wheeled her heavy suitcase through the subway, ignoring the angry looks from people as she took up space they had decided she wasn't entitled too. After the 20 minute trip, she left one platform just to walk to another, feeling surprised that she felt light. It wasn't the fact that all her belongings now fit in one suitcase; it was the feeling of freedom.

Maybe this is what Anna was talking about, Meg thought as she boarded the second train. She put her headphones on and waited the next 30minutes, getting off in the art district and walking up to the street.

All those weight classes turned out to be good for something, Meg thought to herself as she dragged her heavy suitcase up the stairs, silently praying that it didn't break. When she reached the top, she moved to the side and checked her phone, letting it adjust itself before continuing to follow it down the street. Meg found herself in the middle of a place she never dared enter. Not because she felt like she didn't fit in or couldn't afford to live the lifestyle, but because she knew she couldn't. If it hadn't been for Anna's kindness on the plane, there is no way Meg would have continued to search for her apartment building number.

She's not like these snobby bitches, Meg reminded herself, remembering how gentle and tender Anna had been with her, somehow knowing what she needed. Meg stopped out the front of the number 29 Hamilton Avenue and looked up at the building in front of her.

Here goes, Meg thought, walking inside and pressing the elevator button. She rode the elevator up to level 8 and stepped out, walked down the marble corridor until she reached one of the two doors on the level, number 14, and knocked on the door. Meg waited impatiently, her stomach full of knots as she kicked her feet against each other, waiting for Anna to open the door.

"Darling, hello," Anna said, opening the door wide and walking out, embracing Meg and making her laugh.

"Hi, thanks for this," Meg said, feeling embarrassed. Anna shook her head, taking her suitcase and walking it inside.

"Not at all, I'm happy to help, and glad for the company actually," Anna said, allowing herself to give an honest answer.

"Did you find it, ok?" Anna asked, putting Meg's suitcase down by the door and watching as Meg looked around.

"Yeah, it was fine," Meg said, absentmindedly as she looked at the high ceilings and luxury apartment furnishings.

"Your place is average," Meg laughed, teasing Anna and happy when Anna smirked.

"Yeah, it's a little run down, maybe you have some suggestions on how I can fix it," Anna replied, enjoying Meg's humor.

"The guest room is this way," Anna said, taking the suitcase and wheeling it down the hallway. Meg followed, wishing that she could sit down and relax but not wanting to offend Anna. Anna led the way past several rooms, all of which Meg was sure would have also been excellent, stopping when she reached one right at the end of the wide hallway.

"You can stay as long as you need to," Anna said, opening the door and letting Meg walk inside. The room overlooked the park with its floor to ceiling glass wall, the sheer drapes either side adding to the elegance of the room.

"Don't worry about closing them when it's dark, or you get changed, I have a film on them that prevents people from being able to see in during the day and the night," Anna said, sitting on the bed.

"Also, that tablet there turns on the lights, movie screen, and the bathroom is just through those doors," Anna added, continuing to explain the room. Meg was somewhat overwhelmed and began to tear up, trying to hide it but failing to do so.

"Oh, darling, I'm sorry. Is this all too much for you?" Anna said, standing up and walking over to where Meg stood, nodding her head and wiping her tears.

"Come on, come with me, I have something that will cheer you up," Anna said, enjoying being able to take care of the sweet girl. Anna led Meg back out into the living room and sat her down on the couch. She wrapped a heavy, fluffy blanket around her shoulders and poured her a glass of water, tipped some candied dinosaur shapes into a small bowl, and walked back over to Meg. Sitting down on the couch, a seat away, Anna placed everything down on the table and sat back, taking a bite of one of the treats.

"Thanks. You must think I am so weird or something," Meg said, her face blushing red. Here she was, sitting on the couch of a perfect stranger, being looked after because she couldn't get her life in order by herself.

"Not at all, honey," Anna said, reaching out and stroking Meg's cheek lightly.

"I like that," Meg softly said, wishing that her body wasn't betraying her.

Not everything has to be sexual! She thought to herself, wishing that her pussy wasn't getting wet from the attention the attractive woman was giving her.

"I know you do. All little girls do," Anna said, taking a chance but feeling nervous the moment she let the words slip from her lips. Meg looked up at her, fear in her eyes but something else. It wasn't fear of Anna perse. It was fear that Anna saw something in Meg that she tried to hide. Meg tried to speak, but the words didn't seem to want to come out, so she just smiled and rested her head on the back of the couch.

"What do you do for work?" Meg decided to say.

"I'm the CEO of Carson Lighting," Anna said, Meg, opening her eyes suddenly.

"Ok, wow," Meg said, making Anna laugh.

"What?" Anna asked, unsure of what Meg was meaning.

"Like, it's just perfect. Your place, your life, you. Everything is just so perfect," Meg said, wondering how long it would take her to get her life in order.

"Well, not everything is as it seems," Anna said, getting up and getting herself a glass of water.

"No? It looks pretty damn good," Meg said, getting a playful bop on the head.

"Don't say damn," Anna said, enjoying the redness in Meg's cheeks as she was corrected.

"I have all this yes, but I don't have anyone to share it with," Anna said, not wanting to scare Meg off by telling her that she wanted a baby girl to spoil and discipline.

"Is that why you let me crash here?" Meg laughed.

"Well, when you say it like that, it makes me sound desperate," Anna said, rolling her eyes at herself.

"No! I don't think you'd be desperate, look

at you! I bet you could go out and pick up anyone you wanted in like, an hour," Meg exclaimed, making Anna think for a second before smirking at Meg.

"So, where would I go to find a fit, young girl that would want to have mad, passionate sex with me," Anna said, making Meg blush. Anna leaned forward, wrapped her arm around Meg's head, weaving her fingers through her hair. Meg battered her puppy dog eyes and slightly moaned, lifting off the seat as her clit began to throb.

"Yeah, that's what I thought," Anna whispered as she brought her mouth down on top of Meg's, kissing her deeply. Meg moaned into the kiss, finally feeling Anna's touch where she wanted to as the feeling raced to her pussy. Meg slipped her tongue into Anna's mouth, tasting her and pulling the blanket off herself, straddled Anna as she kissed her.

"Yeah?" Anna said as Meg pulled her top off, revealing her perky young breasts. Meg began to grind on top of Anna, making her panties wet.

"Yeah," Meg said, nodding her head, wanting nothing more than to have the woman whose lap she was sitting on, bring her to orgasm. It had been a long time since Meg had been with a woman, finding it hard to find the type of woman she found attractive. If she did find a MILF, they always came with so much baggage that Meg was turned off soon after meeting them. But Anna didn't seem to have any baggage as she shifted positions and lay Meg down on the couch, she knew that she was in for a treat.

"Do you know the traffic light system?" Anna said, reaching up Meg's skirt and feeling her wet slit through her panties. Meg nodded, causing Anna to moan in delight that she didn't have to give the girl a run down.

"Good girl," Anna cooed as Meg spread her thighs for Anna, wanting her touch as desperately as Anna wanted to give it. Anna pulled Meg's panties to the side, enjoying the view of her pink pussy.

"You still shave. I didn't think anyone still

did that," Anna said, making Meg laugh.

"Yeah, I got it lasered like, way back when, so it doesn't grow anymore," Meg said, hoping that it wasn't a deal-breaker for Anna.

"Perfect," Anna said, her mind wandering, thinking of how sweet Meg would always look.

"Such a pretty little girl," Anna said, stopping herself from saying what she wanted to.

Don't call yourself Mommy whatever you do, Anna thought to herself as she tenderly spread Meg's pussy lips, slowing the pace. Meg moaned in frustration at the slowing pace, making Anna laugh.

"Oh, does somebody need to be touched here," Anna said, slapping Megs' pussy with the full palm of her hand and making her yelp.

"I like that sound," Anna said more seriously, spanking her a few more times before finally entering her.

"I just love the feeling of entering you for the first time. So tight, so wet," Anna said as she slowly pushed two fingers inside of Meg, stretching and filling her, making her gasp.

"Good girl, take it from me," Anna said, surprising Meg with how alluring her words were.

Oh fuck, Meg thought as she began to play with her tits as Anna slowly fingered her, pressing on her stomach and making Meg feel every stroke.

"Fuck," Meg gasped, feeling her pussy loosen and her juices beginning to flow more freely. Anna resisted the urge to slap her face, knowing that would be the punishment if she was Anna's baby girl. Instead, Anna pulled out of Meg, stripped herself down until she was wearing just her bra and mid-high pantyhose and black heels.

"Do you know what happens to girls who swear?" Anna said, swinging her panties around one finger. Meg rested on her elbows, biting her bottom lip.

"No," Meg panted, wishing that Anna was still fucking her. Anna bent down over Meg, kissed her cheek, and lovingly stroked her hair before stuffing her panties in her mouth.

"They get gagged," Anna said, making Meg's

cheek burn red as she tasted the woman's sent for the first time. Anna pushed Meg down with her foot, the heel digging into the younger woman's skin, making her cry out.

"Don't worry, baby girl," Anna said, spitting on her hand and going back to work on Meg's cunt.

"I'm not going to hurt you," Anna said, winking at Meg before rubbing her clit with her thumb as her two fingers re-entered Meg's pussy, making her close her eyes and roll her head back.

"Yes, cum for me," Anna said, watching as Meg writhed around on the lounge. The early afternoon sun came through the windows, warming Anna's back as she fucked the young blonde. She loved having Meg at her mercy. She imagined that Meg was already hers.

"Good girl," Anna said, feeling Meg push her hand away and reach up to pull Anna's panties out of her mouth.

There's no way I'd let this happen if you were mine, baby girl, Anna thought as she sat back and let Meg do what she wanted. Meg sat up, took the panties from her mouth, and placed them down on the couch.

"Woah," Meg said, the afterglow of such an intense orgasm flooding her being and making her numb.

"Did you like that?" Anna asked, already knowing the answer.

"Yeah," Meg panted, making Anna laugh.

"What? You think you're done?" Anna questioned, making Meg laugh. Anna grabbed Meg's hair and gently guided her down onto the floor.

"Stick out your tongue," Anna commanded, waiting for Meg to obey her. Anna slowly lowered herself down onto Meg's face, shivering as she felt the girl's wet tongue on her clit, repositioning herself so that it was her pussy that Meg would be tasting.

"Kiss me," Anna said, knowing full well that she wouldn't have to tell the girl how to eat her out, but enjoying doing so nonetheless. Meg obeyed, eating Anna out with a passion she had forgotten she had. Anna moaned and grinded her pussy onto Meg's face, relishing how the girl's tongue never stopped, feeling like a vibrator.

"Such a good girl," Anna moaned, reaching behind her and rubbing Meg's pussy, as Meg made her cum.

"Did I say stop?" Anna said, feeling Meg slow down, waiting for her to get up. Anna smiled as she felt Meg continue to lap up her juices, bringing on another slight orgasm. Anna knew that she wanted more; she wanted to own Meg. She wanted to bend her over, and strap-on fuck her until she was a limp plaything in Anna's arms.

Another time, Anna said to herself, not wanting to scare the girl away. Getting up, Anna laughed a she felt her legs almost give way, sitting on the lounge quickly as she felt the blood begin to flow back through her legs.

"That's what you get for being greedy," Meg laughed, teasing Anna. Anna smirked as she closed her eyes and waited for the pain to leave her body. Meg came up and sat next to Anna, snuggling into her and kissing down her neckline, stopping when she reached her breasts.

"Do you want to see them?" Anna asked, Meg, beginning to blush. She wanted more than just to see them. She wanted to play with them, to suckle on Anna, and to lick her nipples for hours lazily. Meg always felt that she gave herself away whenever she played with a girl's breasts, she could be lost at them for hours and forget all about the sex the other girl thought she was going to get. Meg just blushed and shrugged her shoulders.

"Yeah," Meg said, her little voice escaping, making her blush even more.

"You don't have to, I'm not going to be offended if you don't want to," Anna said, sensing the change in Meg's expression.

"No, I want to," Meg quickly said, making Anna laugh and look at her curiously. Anna slowly took off her red lace bra, exposing her large, heavy breasts, making Meg's clit throb and something inside of her ache.

"They are nice," Meg softly said, reaching

out hesitantly to touch them.

"Here," Anna said, taking Meg's hands and placing them on herself, showing Meg how she liked to be touch.

"They feel so soft," Meg whispered, she bit her bottom lip and Anna decided to take a shot in the dark.

"Do you want to suckle from them?" She asked Meg's reaction all that she needed to know.

"Um, I don't, wouldn't that be weird?" Meg stammered, her face red with a mix of desire and shame.

"What's weird about, a Mommy nursing her baby girl?" Anna said, hoping that she had read Meg right. Meg eyed Anna, her mouth gaped open, and her stomach knotted.

"I thought so," Anna smiled, playing with her breasts. Meg looked down, only looking up when Anna lifted her chin.

"How did you know?" Meg quietly asked, Anna, laughing at the question.

"A good Mommy could see that a mile away.

Plus, the thumb sucking, the cuddly way you wanted me to touch you. You were an easy read," Anna replied, making Meg sigh and look down at her breasts.

"It's been years since I have been with anyone like this," Meg nervously said, feeling out of her depth but wanting Anna with a frenzied desire.

"Then, it's about time you had Mommy take care of you," Anna said, pulling Meg onto her lap and rolling her onto her back. Anna held her breast over Meg's mouth, her nipple touching Meg's lips as she leaned forward.

"Suckle on Mommy, baby girl," Anna said, sending Meg into little space and making her instinctively begin to nurse. Both Meg and Anna moaned in pleasure as Meg started to suckle, Anna feeling her cunt ache.

"Such a good girl," Anna cooed, watching as Meg placed both her hands on her breast and held it in place. Anna reached down to Meg's pussy and began to rub her, smiling as she felt Meg wiggle against her hand.

"Do you like that baby girl?" Anna said, excited that Meg was enjoying herself.

"Yes, Mommy," Meg said, hesitating when she called Anna, Mommy, hoping that Anna didn't mind. The smile on Anna's face told Meg that it was fine.

"Mommy," Meg suddenly moaned, feeling Anna back inside of her.

"What? I told you that I wasn't finished with you," Anna said, quickly finger fucking Meg, loving how she sucked harder the closer she was to orgasm.

"You can't cum sweetie, don't do it," Anna said, making Meg's eyes go wide and hearing her groan in frustration as she was edged. Anna was curious to see how well Meg could control herself.

A little orgasm denial never hurt anyone. Well, mostly, Anna thought to herself, watching how the young girl in her lap gasped and groaned, trying to hold off.

"Wow, Mommy is impressed," Anna said,

raising an eyebrow and watching as Meg continued to writhe under her touch.

"Please, Mommy," Meg moaned in agony, desperate to cum. The sound also made Anna moan and nod her head before she realized she had, only noticing when her fingers were flooded by Meg's juices as she cried out.

"How beautiful," Anna said, knowing that she would have to do everything in her power to keep Meg under her roof and in her bed. Meg just panted as her pussy continued to drip, making Anna smile.

"You know, there's something I could put you in that would keep you pussy juices from messing up your pajama pants," Anna said, hoping that Meg would be down for some Mommy, little playtime. Meg just nodded her head, still in a daze.

"How did I get so lucky to meet you?" Meg softly said, making Anna smile.

"I feel the same way, sweet girl," Anna said, getting up and grabbing Meg's wrist. She didn't want to leave the girl alone and give her the chance to change her mind, and she led her into a room which made Meg stop and freeze on the stop.

"It's the nursey little one," Anna said, watching Meg's face as she pulled her to the floor and onto the changing mat. Anna took out a pacifier, a pink diaper with stars on the front, and a onesie before returning to Meg's side.

"Oh, Mommy," Meg moaned as Anna pushed the pacifier into her mouth and held it in place.

"Don't take it out," Anna instructed, making Meg put her hands back down.

"Good girl," Anna said as she wiped the cum off Meg's pussy and thighs before she powdered her and fastened the diaper. She took the onesie, pulled it over Meg's head, and slid it down her body, smiling at Meg's thin frame.

"Mommy will have to get you something a little bit smaller, won't I?" Anna said. She had onesies in size small and medium, but Meg needed an extra small.

"I still like it, Mommy, it's snuggly," Meg

said, making Anna smile. Meg looked around the nursery, seeing all the toys and then looked back at Anna.

"Do you want to play?" Anna smiled, watching as Meg nodded, and pointed to the stuffie high on the wall. There were three; free-standing shelves mounted to the wall, all of which had a collection of stuffies. Anna smiled and walked over to the top shelf, reached up and took down the cuddly crocodile, and gave it to Meg.

"You are just full of surprises, aren't you?" Anna said, making Meg giggle and nod her head.

"You are a little girl, aren't you, sweetie?" Anna said, noticing that Meg was more and more non-verbal.

"Do you just want to be looked after when you're a little, sweetheart?" Anna said, sitting down on the floor and watching as Meg crawled over to her and sat in her lap.

"Yes, Mommy," Meg said, taking her paci out but putting it back in quickly.

"Well, Mommy can look after you for as

long as you need and want. Does that sound like a plan?" Anna said. Meg's eyes grew wide, and she clapped her hands excitedly.

"This is such a typical lesbian thing to do. Move in together the moment you meet someone," Anna laughed as Meg played with her new stuffie.

Chapter 5

"So I work Monday to Friday, 7-6:30. They are long days. When I come home, I haven't had to worry about anyone but myself for a long time, so it might be a bit rough this week until we come up with a routine," Anna said to Meg the following morning over brunch. Anna had taken Meg out to a fancy brunch bar, and the two of them were waiting for their meals. Anna liked that Meg had ordered something healthy.

"Ok. They are long days," Meg said, wondering what she would do for all the time that she would be in the apartment alone.

"Tell me about your job?" Anna asked, her fruit platter being put down in front of her. Meg waited until her meal was also placed down before answering the question.

"Well. I am a freelance graphic designer. So I make book covers, a few logos, but mostly book covers," Meg replied, impressing Anna.

"You don't look old enough to have a degree," Anna said, smirking, clearly teasing Meg.

"I'm 26!" Meg said, taking the bait.

"Oh, that's endearing," Anna replied, loving how enthusiastically Meg had replied.

"How old are you?" Meg quietly asked, making Anna laugh.

"Older than 26," Anna replied, making Meg roll her eyes.

"I'm 45, my birthday is in a few months," Anna more seriously replied. Meg took no time at all to do the math.

"Ok, cool," Meg said, trying not to laugh, Anna never missing a beat.

"You laugh now, but let's see you at 45 missy," she said, playfully kicking Meg under the table, surprising her.

"I didn't say anything!" Meg insisted, Anna not believing her for a second.

"Ok, so. I usually get up at like 8, make a coffee and begin working until like 12, have lunch and finish for the day at 4, got for a run till five, and then chill out till 10 when I go to bed," Meg explained.

"Yeah, so I would have already been gone by the time you've woken up, and my day is over long after yours. I don't get home until 6:30, and I'm out of the house in the morning by 6:30," Anna said, feeling disappointed that her workdays were so long. Her schedule had been a deal-breaker for so many girls in the past. She hadn't realized until that very moment that she had given up looking for a permanent girlfriend.

"That's ok. I can maybe just run with your schedule for like a week and see how we go? I'd get so much work done!" Meg giggled as she finished her brunch, sipping the champagne and looking around the space. The room was filled with the type of fancy people who always had looked down on her growing up. She had come from a hard-working, middle-class family who tried their best to put her through good schools. The problem was, that was all her parents could afford. They couldn't provide the money for the class trips, brand new uniforms, or money to do things with her friends on the weekends and over the summer. Very quickly, she was deemed a loser who none of the other girls wanted to be around. Sure she got a great education, but the cruel remarks and social isolation that she experienced still haunted her. Shaking off the thought, she looked back at Anna, who had been watching her.

"You're uncomfortable here," Anna said, rather than asked, tilting her head knowingly when Meg tried to dispute her remark.

"It's not that. It's just. I've never been good enough for these types of people," Meg said, feeling embarrassed that she let others take her power away so easily. She had always done that. She didn't seem to know how to stop it, that was what annoyed her.

"Hmm, let's go somewhere that you like then," Anna said, getting up and taking her glass of champagne with her.

"Can you leave with that?" Meg whispered

as they made their way out the door.

"Darling, Mommy can do whatever the hell I want," Anna said, enjoying how the young girl looking up at her made her feel.

"Don't swear, Mommy," Meg teased, coping a playful spanking on her ass.

"So, where are you taking me?" Anna said, dropping her champagne glass in the sidewalk bin and reaching for Meg's hand.

"So, there's this place, it's a little run-down, but they sell great sweet treats. It's by the river," Meg explained. She loved how people got out of Anna's, and therefore, her way as they walked. Usually, Meg had to scramble through the masses, but with Anna, they seemed to part and made her way clear.

"I will have to remember that you can eat like a frat boy and still have that perfect body. Enjoy that, it goes, trust me," Anna said, making Meg laugh. They walked the three blocks, made a left turn, and head down to the water.

"You're right, this isn't my scene," Anna

said, feeling vulnerable.

"Don't worry, I got you," Meg said, looking up at her. Anna reached out and touched Meg's face affectionately just as two guys entered the alley from behind them. Two other men then entered from the other side, and Anna felt her grip tighten on Meg's hand.

"It's ok Mommy, I'm not going to let anything bad happen to you," Meg said reassuringly. Anna wanted to believe her, but as the men got closer, she wasn't so sure.

"Give me your wallet," one of the men said, taking out a gun and pointing it at Anna.

"She doesn't have the wallets, I do," Meg said, stepping forward. She looked around. Her parents owned a Krav Maga studio on the Westside, hardly the lucrative money machine, but it had taught her a thing or two. She knew that the guy with the gun was the only one she needed to worry about, the other three would run away the minute she had the gun in her hands. Meg slowly pushed Anna behind her and reached into her jacket pocket. She could tell the man with the gun was in a rush by the way he kept looking around, and as he looked over his shoulder, Meg quickly disarmed him and shot into the air above her head.

"Get out of here, or the next one is for you," she said, slowly bringing her arm down and pointing the gun at the leader's face and putting her finger back on the trigger.

"Run," Meg said, stepping forward and watching as the men scrambled back up the hill and out onto the street and disappearing. Meg turned back to Anna, who was in shock.

"Right, well, I will be tying you up if I ever have to punish you!" Anna said, making Meg laugh.

"I'm not like that all the time, just when I have to be," Meg said, shaking her head.

"Yeah, I see that," Anna said, taking the gun out of Meg's hand and putting the safety on before putting it in her handbag.

"I thought you were going to throw it in the river," Meg laughed.

"No, I want to take it to the police. Who

knows the horrible things those men have done. If there is a chance they can get caught, I want the police to be able to have that chance," Anna said, following Meg into a shop with a wooden door. Inside the shop, Anna smelt the sweet smell of candy from her childhood.

"Oh, you are such a clever little girl," Anna said as she saw the candy-filled jars behind the counter.

"Hi, how's it going?" The man behind the counter asked. He had that; old grandfather look about himself. The tall, jolly-looking man with a big beard and a white apron, the red and white stripe of his shirt made Meg smile.

"I haven't seen you in here for a while, Meggsy," the man said, making Anna raise an eyebrow.

"Meggsy?" Anna questioned, finding the name endearing but also somewhat disturbing.

"Anna, this is Phil. Phil, Anna," Meg said, introducing the two. Phil smiled warmly, came around the counter, and shook hands with Anna.

"It's a pleasure to meet you. Meggsy used to come here when she was a kid and stayed for hours. I gave her her first job because by the time she could work, she knew everything by heart," Phil said, the chuckle he had at the end of the sentence making his cheeks rosy.

"I love that. That's so sweet," Anna said, looking at Meg, who was smiling bashfully.

"We'll take two of everything from the top shelf," Meg said, turning to Phil, who was already making his way back behind the counter.

"Always the same," Phil teased.

"This used to be Meggsy's standard order back in the day," Phil said, filling two red and white striped paper bags.

"Thank you for taking me here," Anna said, enjoying the intimate act of letting her into Meg's world. Meg just gave her a sideward smile before trying to pay Phil, who declined.

"On the house," he said, waving his hands at her.

"Well, then, take the tip," Meg said, putting

the money in the tip jar before hurrying out of the store laughing as Phil continued to try and protest.

"You are going to need to brush your teeth extra well tonight, young lady," Anna said, taking a bite of the pink sugar crystal-coated marshmallow and moaned in delight.

"I know right, pretty yummy," Meg said, tasting the smooth chocolate of her liquid caramel, chocolate shelled ball.

They walked back up to the street, straight to the police station and handed the gun in. Both Meg and Anna had to make a statement about how the weapon came to be in their possession and were walking back to Anna's apartment by 4 o'clock.

"What do you want to do now?" Meg said, holding onto Anna's hand like she hadn't only met her less than 48 hours earlier. Anna thought for a moment.

What I need to do is check my emails and go grocery shopping so I can meal prep for the week. Then I need to go to the gym and burn off all these calories. I wanted to go to the sauna as well, Anna thought to herself.

"I don't know, I had nothing planned," Anna decided to say instead, enjoying the feeling of spontaneity. They turned the corner and continued to walk, both yawning at the same time.

"I think I am about to be in a sugar coma," Meg laughed, causing Anna to reach down, take her paper bag and put it in her handbag.

"That's enough for you then," Anna said, an idea crossing her mind.

"Do you like the gym?" Anna asked, walking past the doorman and into the elevator.

"I guess. I don't have a membership to one or anything like that, though," Meg replied.

"The apartment has a gym, as well as a sauna. Want to go work out for a while?" Anna suggested. Meg couldn't remember the last time she worked out but shrugged her shoulders and nodded her head.

"Ok great," Anna said, opening the door to her home. Meg walked to her room, changed into something she was happy to exercise in, and made her way back to the living room to wait for Anna. She took out her phone while she waited, instantly regretting the choice.

Baby, I'm sorry. I made a huge mistake that I want to spend the rest of my life making up to you. You deserve so much better than me. I want to get professional help so that I can be the man you deserve, came the onslaught of messages from her ex. Meg turned her phone off before looking around the apartment and shaking her head.

This is what I deserve. Not some fuckboy who couldn't keep it in his pants, Meg thought to herself, jumping up when she heard Anna coming down the hall.

"Ready?" Anna asked, sitting on a chair and tying her shoes. Meg left her phone on the lounge.

"Yep," she replied, brushing off Anna's curious look.

"Wait. Tell me what's going on," Anna said, making Meg annoyed that she could tell something was up.

"Nothing," Meg said, trying to walk to the door, just to have Anna grab her wrist.

"Sweetie, don't lie to me," Anna loving said, bringing Meg into her arms and wrapping them around her.

"How can you do that?" Meg said in frustration, making Anna smile to herself knowingly.

"Because Mommy always knows," Anna said, taking Meg to the couch and sitting her down.

"It's just Alex. He messaged me a whole bunch of texts saying how he is going to change and that he is sorry, and it just makes me so mad that I could have stayed with somebody so pathetic," Meg said, Anna, giving her her undivided attention.

"You don't need to be angry with yourself," Anna said, Meg, sighing and moving closer to cuddle into Anna.

"I'm happy that he kicked me out because if it hadn't been for him doing it, I would probably still be with the loser. When I could have been here with you for all this time," Meg said, hoping that Anna didn't think she was pathetic for sharing her feelings.

"It's just, I've never had somebody care for the way you seem to," Meg said, looking down, embarrassed that she felt so deeply so quickly.

"He will probably keep messaging you. Have you thought about blocking his number?" Anna suggested, Meg, shaking her head.

"May I then?" Anna said, holding out her hand to Meg and waiting for Meg to hand her the phone. Anna swiped a few times, finding his name and holding the phone up for Meg to see, watching her face as she blocked his number and then deleted it from her phone.

"There, Mommy made it all better," Anna said, rocking Meg in her arms.

Chapter 6

Anna's 5:30 alarm went off in the morning, unbeknownst to Meg, who had slept in the guest room Sunday night. Anna quietly walked around the apartment as she got ready, but the smell of her freshly made cappuccino woke Meg.

"Hi baby girl," Anna said, her appearance taking Meg by surprise.

"Oh my god, you're beautiful," Meg said, rubbing her eyes and trying to focus them. Anna wore her black heels, black pantyhose, a stylish black dress with a crisp white shirt underneath, a tan cape-scarf, and an elegant, bridle style black and brushed gold metal belt which clinched at her waist. Her makeup was flawless, her thick, wavy brown hair looked like it had been freshly blown out and as she stood with her cappuccino in one hand, and her other on her hip. She looked like a goddess.

"I'm happy you approve," Anna smirked, knowing that she looked amazing. Meg looked down at her pajamas, ran her fingers through somewhat messy blonde hair, and then looked back up at Anna.

"Oh, baby girl, you aren't meant to look like me," Anna said, checking her Rolex and sighing, knowing that her car and driver would be waiting downstairs for her.

"Mommy loves how little you look. But I have to go. There's food in the fridge, make yourself at home," Anna said, embracing Meg, kissing her passionately and grabbing her ass before she pulled herself away from the girl. She groaned in frustration at not having more time with her new favorite person before heading out the door and leaving Meg alone and standing in the spacious but empty apartment.

Well, now what? Meg thought, checking the time. She shrugged her shoulders, decided to make herself a coffee.

I can see how she found it hard to keep a girl

around. Meg thought as she took her coffee outside and looked over the city. Sure, Anna's life was beautiful, she could buy anything she wanted, she could have anyone she wanted, but it came at a huge cost, and that cost was time.

I guess I just need to find my passions and get used to spending a lot of my time during the week without her. I'm sure I could get used to this, I got used to living with a lying dirtbag, this is an upgrade, Meg thought as she watched the city slowly come to life.

"Hi, baby girl, how are you?" Anna said down the phone. It was 3 in the afternoon, and Meg had been online all day.

"Hey, really good, I have so many things to tell you when you get home," Meg excitedly said.

"I can't wait to hear. I just wanted to check in to make sure you were ok," Anna said, silencing the person who came to her door.

"But I have to go now honey, I'll see you tonight," Anna said, hanging up the phone quickly.

"Lol, bye then," Meg said out loud before going back to her laptop.

"Honey, Mommy's home," Anna said at 7 pm. Although the drive to her office was just over half an hour in the mornings, it was less than 15 minutes during the evening.

"Sorry I'm late, I had to pick a few things up from the store. I could have gotten my assistant to do it for me, but I just love the feeling for doing a quick grocery shop," Anna said, smiling when she saw Meg in the living room.

"That's fine. What did you get?" Meg asked, her stomach growling.

"Oh, baby!" Anna said, coming to sit down next to her and rubbing her tummy.

"Mommy will get you a bottle, and that should keep you going until dinner," Anna said, kissing Meg on the head before standing back up and holding out her hand.

"Come on," she said, waiting for Meg to obey her, smiling when she did so.

"I bought some duck, some seasonal vegetables, and a herb rub I thought would be nice. It won't take me very long to make this all up," Anna said, sitting Meg down and beginning to make her a protein shake.

"Yummy," Meg said, making Anna smirk.

"I thought my little, sweet tooth would like it," Anna said, handing Meg the bottle.

"Tell Mommy about your day," Anna said, putting her hair up and rolling up her sleeves.

"So! I did some cool things," Meg said, her eyes sparkling.

"I made up a timetable of all the stuff I can do while you're at work so that I am not just waiting around losing my mind," Meg explained, making Anna laugh.

"Good. Keep going," Anna said, taking out pots and pans.

"So, I have a work schedule, I work 9 hours a day now, three hours on, half an hour off and I start this at 6:30 when you leave. I thought it might be nice to wake up together, you know, to have a little morning kiss," Meg said, Anna, coming behind her.

"Or a little morning fuck," Anna said, rubbing over Megs' breasts as she passed.

"Or that," Meg laughed.

"Then at 4:30, I head to the library because at five they have book readings. I don't care which book it is. I just thought it might be nice to hear that. Then after at 5:30, I go do something different each day until 6:30, and we get home at pretty much the same time," Meg said, feeling very proud of herself.

"My clever girl," Anna said, pouring herself a glass of rose wine as Meg handed her her bottle.

"I'm finished, Mommy," Meg said, Anna, taking the bottle and putting it in the dishwasher.

"I love that you have done this, it makes me feel like you want to be with me and I love that," Anna said, putting the duck and vegetables in the roasting pan before putting it in the oven.

"I do want to be with you," Meg said, lovingly smiling at Anna.

"Let's get you all cleaned up and out of those big girl clothes," Anna said, making Meg laugh.

"I don't feel very little night," Meg said, Anna, smirking.

"Oh, you will," Anna said, tickling Meg and making her squeal and run up the hallway toward the bathroom.

Anna ran Meg a bath, putting in bath toys, bubbles, and lighting some sweet-smelling candles.

"Armies up," Anna said, Meg, obeying her immediately.

She might have been right about me feeling little, Meg thought to herself, feeling her little self coming out with each passing second. Anna took off Meg's bra, frowning as she saw the bra lines.

"Mommy is going to take you shopping on the weekend for new bras, I don't like that they cut into you like this," Anna said, running her fingers over Meg's skin, the touch painful, making Meg flinch.

"Ok, Mommy," Meg said as Anna helped her into the huge bathtub. Giggling, Meg ducked her head under the water, loving that the bath was more like a mini swimming pool.

"This is so nice!" Meg exclaimed, scooping up a handful of bubbles and blowing them in the air before laying back down in the warm water.

"Mommy's happy little girl," Anna softly said as she slowly undressed. She liked the way Meg's eyes were always glued on her when she was naked.

"Can Mommy join you, baby girl?" Anna asked, getting into the tub as Meg nodded.

"Oh, there she is," Anna said, enjoying how Meg became quiet, swimming over to her and cuddling in her lap.

"Cuddly baby," Anna said, holding onto Meg and sitting in the shallow end of the tub. Anna loved feeling Meg resting her head on her ample breasts, the water lapping just under her nipples.

"I love you, Mommy," Meg involuntarily sighed, darting upright and looking Anna fearfully in the eye.

"It's ok little one, Mommy isn't freaked out about that," Anna said, Meg, beginning to suck her thumb.

"You're not?" Meg asked, her eyes as wide as ever.

"No. I think, when it's right, it's right. And I feel so alive when I am with you. It is probably a lot to do with the fact that we just met and everything is new and exciting, but I also think that it is because of how open we have been with and to each other. I have never had a baby girl who has been as independent as you without being a little brat. I love that you let me look after you but, at the same time, spent the day making sure to look after yourself as well. You are the type of woman I have been looking for," Anna said, the smile on Meg's face said enough.

"Oh, Mommy," Meg said, burying her face in Anna's cleavage, just for Anna to reposition her in her arms and bring her nipple up to Meg's lips.

"Suckle on Mommy, little girl," Anna said,

bringing Meg's head closer to her thick, hard nipple, smiling and happily sighing when Meg began to obey her.

"Good girl," Anna said, closing her eyes and resting her head on the towel she had positioned at the end of the tub. As Meg suckled, Anna thought back to their dinner in the oven and knew that they needed to get out of the tub shortly, but looking down to see Meg's wide eyes looking up at her, her lips pursed around Anna's breast and her hand grabbing onto Anna's body, Anna would have much rather stayed in that position until the water was freezing cold.

This is what I needed, Anna thought to herself. The emotional release she experienced having Meg on her breasts was something she knew she would never want to live without ever again. Patting Meg gently on her ass and placing her hands under Meg's arms, lifting her off, Anna stood up.

"We need to get in some warm jammies, baby girl," Anna explained as Meg whined, pouted and reached for Anna. Looking down into the water, Meg nodded her head, making Anna smile, enjoying being craved as much as Meg craved her.

"Don't worry. You can have more Mommy cuddles before bed. But we will get sick if we stay in here for too much longer, sick and hungry," Anna lovingly explained, standing up and getting out of the tub, she guided Meg out and dried her off.

"I don't want you to crawl to the nursery, baby girl. The marble might be too painful on your little knees," Anna said as Meg got to the floor.

"But I'm tired, Mommy," Meg softly whined, rubbing her eyes, making Anna smile.

"I know, just a little bit longer, baby girl," Anna said, taking Meg's hand and leading her to the nursery.

"Lay down, honey," Anna said when they finally reached the nursery. Meg could smell the crispy duck and sweet vegetables in the oven, making her stomach growl and Anna laugh.

"Soon, little one. Let Mommy get you

dressed and then you can have yummy dinner and play or cuddle until bedtime," Anna said as she took out a diaper and a thick pad, sticking it onto the diaper before coming back down to the changing mat on the floor. Meg had found an aquarium mat and was busy kicking her legs in the air as she lay on her tummy and pushed the fish around.

"Rollover for me," Anna said, taking Meg's hips in her hands and turning her over, only for Meg to resist and try to roll back.

"Not, a good idea," Anna sternly said, reaching down and taking Meg's chin in her hand and making her look at her dead in the eye. Meg looked down in submission before Anna let her go and began to diaper her, making sure the diaper was on tight. Meg could feel the pad pressing into her pussy. Anna had made sure of that by opening Meg's pussy lips as she diapered her, knowing that it would rub on her clit.

"The more you wriggle, the more it'll rub," Anna said, pushing a paci into Meg's mouth as she rubbed her between her legs. Going back to the cupboard, Anna took out a matching set of duck pajamas as a pair of fluffy yellow socks. Meg giggled as she saw the outfit, clapping her hands and helping Anna as she got dressed.

"What a sweet little girl," Anna said, sitting back and looking at the adorable blonde playing in front of her.

"Mommy?" Meg questioned as she heard Anna leaving the room.

"Mommy is going to get out of this robe and into something more snuggly. Then we are going to have dinner. I'll come and get you after I'm dressed," Anna said, knowing what Meg's concern was before she even had to say it out loud. Meg smiled behind her paci before turning back around and continued to play. Anna left the room, hearing the timer go off on the oven, she walked to the kitchen and took their dinner out, leaving it to sit on the bench as she went back into her room to get dressed. She loved that Meg was so easily pleased that she was no trouble and was happy to be babied the way Anna liked. Anna hung her robe on the wall of her walk-in cupboard and walked around the room to where she kept her pajamas. Given, they were more her house clothes than pajamas as she preferred to sleep with only her panties on. She took out a pair of designer navy sweat pants and a white racerback singlet, her large, natural aesthetically looking yet fake breasts pressing the material out, making her smile. She took her hair out, put on some warm socks, and walked back out to find Meg sitting in the living room floor crying.

"Baby girl, what has happened?" Anna said, rushing over and bending down to see Meg clutching her foot.

"I hurt it, Mommy," Meg said, taking her hands away slightly, to show Anna. Anna gasped as she saw the small amount of blood coming through the sock.

"Baby, how?" Anna said, kissing Meg's cheeks before standing up and going to get her medical supplies, coming back almost instantly.

"I dropped my phone on it," Meg said, pointing to her phone, the shattered screen coming from it landing on the floor after it had cut Meg's foot.

"Oh, little one," Anna said, taking Meg's sock off slowly and cleaning her small wound.

"It's ok, little one, Mommy is here, I'll look after you," Anna cooed, wrapping Meg's toe in a bandage and going back to the nursery to take out another pair of socks.

"I'm sorry, Mommy," Meg said, beginning to cry again, worried that Anna would be angry with her for ruining her things.

"You don't need to be sorry, Mommy isn't mad at all, little girl!" Anna exclaimed, helping Meg over to the dining room table before placing her plate of food down in front of her.

"I cut it up for you, do you want me to feed you or do you want to do it yourself," Anna asked, sipping her wine.

"I can do it!" Meg proudly said, looking at Anna, making sure it was ok to start eating.

"Alright, sweet girl," Anna said, stroking Meg's cheek and beginning to eat.

After dinner, Anna took Meg back down to the floor, setting her up with the aqua mat, some blocks, and her crocodile stuffie she had name Sven.

"Mommy is going to tidy the kitchen. Then I want to have some chill-out time on the couch before bed, alright? Are you happy to keep playing there?" Anna asked from the kitchen, content with Meg's nod, and began packing the dishes into the dishwasher. Coming down to the lounge area, Anna poured herself another glass of wine, and began to scroll through her phone, checking her social media accounts and messaging with friends as Meg build Sven a castle.

Does it get any better than this!? Anna thought to herself, watching Meg play.

Chapter 7

At 9:45, Anna yawned and lay down on the couch. Meg turned around, looking at Anna, who was sleepily smiling and watching her.

"Mommy, is it bedtime?" Meg asked, resting her head on the couch close to Anna's face. Anna leaned forward, kissed Meg on the nose, and nodded her head.

"Yes, but I don't want the day to be over," Anna said, pulling Meg onto her and stroking her hair as Meg rested on Anna's breasts.

"But we can just do it all again tomorrow, can't we?" Meg questioned, feeling Anna's legs wrap around her.

"Yes," Anna replied, patting Meg's padded bottom and smiling.

"So, are you going to get up with Mommy tomorrow morning? Do you want me to undress you, or do you want to do that yourself? Mommy is going to go to the gym after work tomorrow. You can come down if you like?" Anna said, covering Meg's forehead with kisses.

"I can do it. I think that if I'm going to have such long days, I only want to be little in the night time. I can't be little and try to go out into the city, Mommy, I'll get lost!" Meg replied, making Anna laugh.

"And, yeah, I'll come to the gym with you," Meg added, Anna, smiling and indicating that she wanted Meg to sit up by the head tilt she gave her.

"Time for teethies and then bed," Anna said. She wondered if Meg would want to continue to sleep in her bed or if she would feel comfortable sleeping in Anna's.

You met her 48 hours ago. You've fucked her, regressed her, and let her move in with you, and you're nervous about asking her if she wants to sleep in your bed? Anna thought to herself, laughing out loud at how crazy her time with Meg had been.

"You're going to sleep in Mommy's bed

from now on, alright, little one?" Anna said, smiling when Meg threw her arms around Anna's waist and held her tight.

"I am so happy you said that, Mommy," Meg said, letting her go as they reached the bathroom. They cleaned, flossed, and used mouthwash before they left, Meg watching as Anna put on night cream.

"This is how Mommy stays looking so good," Anna said, making Meg laugh. Anna then took Meg's hand and led her up into her bed, going back into the living room to get Sven before tucking Meg in next to her.

"Goodnight, little one," Anna said, kissing Meg on both her cheeks before letting her snuggle in close as they fell asleep.

The alarm woke Meg up with a start, making Anna laugh.

"Oh, baby girl, it might take some getting used to," she said, laughing. Meg looked around the room, one of the walls coming to life with a rainforest backdrop and birds flying across the screen.

"It's a virtual reality wall," Anna explained as Meg watched in awe.

"Of course it is," Meg laughed. She yawned, stretched, and looked down at her clothes and sighed.

"Don't worry. You'll be Mommy's little girl again soon enough," Anna said, kissing her forehead and beginning to unbutton her pajama shirt.

"Hey, I can do it!" Meg playfully exclaimed as she wriggled away from Anna, who just raised her eyebrow and smirked.

"Alright, then. Coffee and toast?" Anna asked as she walked into the cupboard, seeing Meg nod her head before she disappeared. Meg took off her pajamas and diaper, shaking her head almost as if to activate her adult self once more.

"So. What activity are you going to do today after the library?" Anna asked. Today was the first day Meg would put her schedule into place, hoping that she had given herself enough variety and breaks that it kept her well-paced and entertained. Today was Tuesday, and she had planned to go to an art gallery for an hour after the library.

"I'm going to the art gallery. I have no idea what's in there, but it's what I'm doing," Meg said, before running down the hallway, limping on her foot. She had forgotten all about her sore toe and moaned in frustration that it hurt. She put on a pair of jeans, her oversized cable knit sweater, and put her hair up in a messy bun, adding glasses to her look.

"Don't you look like an absolute picture," Anna said, coming out, enjoying the gaped mouth response Meg gave her.

"Nothing compared to that," Meg replied, looking Anna up and down.

"I wouldn't feel like you were my baby girl if you looked like Mommy," Anna said, making Meg her breakfast. Anna wore a tight pair of cropped blue jeans, a loose white silk blouse, and a long, light pink coat she wore open. She had a matching handbag and a Chanel brooch on her coat, her hair as immaculate as ever.

"Can you go into my room and get Mommy's cream, Fendi pumps, baby girl?" Anna said, buttering Meg's toast. Meg rushed down from her stool, and walked to the shoe cupboard, took out the heels Anna was referring to before coming back, and opening her mouth as Anna fed her a mouthful of toast.

"Thank you, baby," Anna seductively said, watching as Meg ate. Another alarm went off, Anna rolling her eyes and quickly put her heels on.

"Bye-bye honey," she said, kissing Meg's lips, enjoying the salty, buttering taste of Meg's mouth and getting lost in the kiss before Meg pushed her away.

"You're going to be late," Meg laughed, watching as Anna came back for more.

"Fuck em," Anna said, putting her handbag down on the bench and wrapped Meg up in her arms as she passionately kissed her.

"I want that pussy tonight," Anna said,

groping Meg's body, eliciting moans of pleasure from the girl.

"That's what I needed to get through this day," Anna laughed, stealing a few more quick kisses before walking to the door, turning back to face Meg and shaking her tits for her before she left the apartment.

"It's surprisingly easy and productive," Meg said down the phone as she made lunch.

"Good, I don't want this to be hard for you," Anna replied. She was on her lunch break and decided to call Meg after not hearing from her all day. She liked that Meg understood that Anna couldn't give her her undivided attention while she was at work. So many of her ex's had hated that when Anna was at work, she didn't want anything to distract her, which meant that they had to wait.

"I've only got a few more orders to do, and then I'm done for the day. I didn't think that I would be able to get through things so quickly but, here we are," Meg said. She had cooked a piece of salmon and a salad for herself, enjoying the array of ingredients in Anna's pantry and fridge.

"Have you thought about what you want to do when you have finished everything?" Anna said, eating the meal her assistant had picked up for her. A steak from one of the most famous steak houses in the city.

"Yes, Netflix!" Meg replied, making Anna laugh. She had half expected the girl to say, researching for new cover ideas, or upskilling but she smiled and appreciated that Meg was young.

"Oh, my sweet girl," Anna said, remembering just how sweet Meg was and licking her lips as she thought about the sex she was going to have that night.

"Well, my perfect girl, Mommy, has to get back to work. So I'll see you tonight. Don't forget. We are going to the gym together," Anna said, hanging up the phone. She was sure it was a power thing, to have the last word, but she loved that Meg didn't seem to mind that she always ended their conversations abruptly.

"See you then," Meg replied to herself, smiling as she continued her lunch.

Meg was already waiting for Anna in the gym. She walked on the treadmill as she watched a movie on her phone. Feeling the firm slap on her ass, she pulled her headphones down around her neck to see Anna standing behind her, smiling.

"Hey sugar," Anna said, the clear lustful look in her eye telling Meg that she wasn't only going to be Anna's baby tonight.

"Hey Mommy," Meg said, jumping down and hugging the taller woman.

"You look cute," Anna said, noting Meg's gray fitness tights, her pink t-shirt, and a gray sweater wrapped around her hips.

"Thanks," Meg beamed, as Anna go on the treadmill next to her.

"Wanna race?" Anna challenged, the look in Meg's eyes encouraging.

"I think I'd win," Meg teased, delighting

Anna.

"Well, let's find out," Anna said, putting her machine up to level 12, only for Meg to do the same.

"Winner is the one who stays on the longest," Anna said, making Meg laugh.

"And every five minutes we go up a level," Meg added, surprising Anna.

"Alright, little one, let's see what you got," Anna said, beginning to run. Meg giggled as she ran, only becoming serious a few minutes in, deciding that she didn't want Anna to win. Anna, who thought this would be an easy win, felt her lungs heave as Meg's young, thin body seemed to float with each step.

"I ran track in school," Meg said, panting only slightly.

"Yes, but school for you was about two minutes ago. I ran track in school too, but that was a long time ago," Anna panted, refusing to give up as they upped the level.

"You're so stubborn," Meg said, wishing

that Anna would let her win. Her toe had started to hurt, and she didn't know how much longer she could maintain the pace.

"I could say the same thing about you!" Anna exclaimed, reaching out to slap Meg on the ass. Meg laughed, coughing slightly and accepted defeat, stopping her machine.

"You. Win," Meg panted, Anna, stopping her machine and pacing around the room with her hands on her head.

"Yeah, but you didn't make it easy," Anna said, taking a sip of water from her bottle.

"Here," Anna said, noticing that Meg didn't have any water with her. Meg gratefully took the bottle and guzzled half before handing it back.

"So, I didn't tell you what the winner gets," Anna said, taking off her shoes and shirt, standing in front of Meg in just her tights and sports bra. Her flat but soft tummy glistened, her full breasts looked amazing in her sports crop.

"I think I can guess," Meg said, taking her shoes off.

"I told the front desk to reserve the gym for us," Anna said, taking Meg's hand and leading her to the weights room where she laid down an extra big towel and pushed Meg down.

"Stay," Anna said, taking her hair out and swaying her head a few times to loosen her wavy mane.

"I know that little body of yours will be tired, but you're going to have to keep going for Mommy, do you understand?" Anna said, feeling herself becoming particularly predatory toward Meg as she looked at her laying on the floor as Anna fastened her strap on harness in place.

"Mommy is going to make you cum until the pretty, slutty little body of yours can do nothing but lay there and take it, that pretty pussy leaking as you lay used and spent," Anna said stroking the cock as she bent her knees and knelt above Meg's face. Turning over, Meg felt the silicone push past her lips, making her gag.

"Such a pretty little sight to see," Anna moaned, stroking Meg's hair and pushing herself further into Meg's throat.

"You'll learn," Anna said, placing her hand along Meg's throat and feeling how closed it was.

"You need to relax it," Anna said, guiding Meg gently as she pulled back just to slowly push forward once again, smiling as she felt Meg's throat open a little bit more.

"Just like that," Anna said, continuing to train her. Meg's eyes watered as she took Anna, gasping every time she pulled back, shaking her head, and not wanting anymore.

"Shh, you're ok," Anna said, holding Meg in her arms and rocking her gently.

"I'm going to stick it somewhere else now, are you going to be a good little whore for Mommy?" Anna questioned, laying Meg on her back and bringing her knees up to her chest.

"Yes, Mommy," Meg said, feeling her body accept Anna's thick cock, gasping in surprise.

"Did you think you'd be able to stop me, laying in this position?" Anna laughed as she filled Meg and held herself balls deep inside of her as she spoke.

"Nothing you do will be able to stop Mommy," Anna said, beginning to fuck Meg aggressively.

"I want to fucking own this cunt," Anna said, reaching down and pinching Meg's nipples, feeling the girl underneath her drip her cum onto Anna's thighs.

"Yes, Mommy's horny little girl," Anna said, pulling out of Meg, whose cunt leaked down her ass cheeks and onto the towel.

"Get your ass over here," Anna aggressively said as she sat on a bench, her cock sticking out and glistening in Meg's cum.

"Mommy, I'm tired," Meg whined, making Anna's clit throb.

"Oh, I know you are," Anna replied, taking Meg's wrists in her hands and turning the girl around, facing away from her.

"But that doesn't mean I am," Anna said, pulling Meg onto her lap and pushing her hips forward, spearing her cunt with her cock.

"Bounce on Mommy's cock," Anna said, watching as Meg strained to obey her but finding it hard as Anna continued to pull her arms back.

"Good girl," Anna said, beginning to bounce Meg on her lap herself.

"You like that, don't you, getting fucked like the whore you are. Mommy's little whore," Anna said, feeling herself cumming as the harness rubbed against her clit. She wrapped her arms around Meg, pushed her back to the floor and mounted her from behind, relishing the fact that she had to hold Meg up to stop her from collapsing on the floor.

"Just take it," Anna demanded as she pounded into Meg, making herself and Meg cum in unison before putting her down gently on the towel and pulling out of her. Anna smirked as she undid her harness, let it fall to the ground, enjoying Meg flinch as it landed close to her.

"Are you alright?" Anna said, lying down next to Meg, who was sucking her thumb. Anna and Meg had discussed tonight's sex scene, but it had felt different from how Meg had thought it would feel.

"Yep," Meg softly said, as she turned away from Anna.

"Hey. Don't run away from me. Talk to me," Anna said, Meg, turning back to look at her, her eyes filling with tears.

"I don't want to be a whore," Meg said, her tears rolling down her cheeks.

"Oh, sweetie," Anna said, sitting up and pulling Meg into her lap, wrapping her arms around her and holding her in a loving embrace.

"I'm so sorry, baby girl," Anna said, wishing that she had known that Meg had reached her limit and feeling awful.

"I'll never call you that again, sweetie," Anna said, reaching for Meg's hoodie and wrapping it around her body.

"I'm sorry I didn't notice it was affecting you. Why didn't you tell me?" Anna asked, holding Meg close to her breasts.

"Because I wanted to please you," Meg

softly said, looking up at Anna.

"But it doesn't baby girl. You putting yourself in situations that you don't like doesn't please me at all. In fact, I feel the opposite," Anna explained, making Meg cry again and bury her face in Anna's breasts.

"Oh, my silly little girl," Anna said, rocking Meg in her arms until she settled.

"Let's go upstairs and get you all clean and settled," Anna said once Meg had stopped crying. Meg nodded and put her clothes back on, followed Anna in silence back up to the apartment and took a shower by herself. Coming out, she put on her pajamas and sat on the lounge where Anna was waiting for her.

"Do you know what you need? Can you tell me how I can make you feel better?" Anna asked. She had also showered and sitting in her normal house clothes. Meg smirked, knowing exactly what she needed and wanted, nodding her head.

"Well? Tell Mommy," Anna said, tilting her

head down to meet Meg's gaze.

"I want to be mean to you," Meg softly said, Anna laughing, looking up at the ceiling and nodding her head as she looked back at Meg.

"Alright. Give me your best," Anna said, making Meg laugh.

"Come on. Tell me what you need to, that Mommy is a bitch, that I hurt your feelings," Anna said, sitting up tickling Meg.

"That you're the whore," Meg said, making Anna gasp and look at her wide-eyed in amusement.

"Ok, there you go," Anna said. She was so surprised by how she was reacting.

Wow, the old me would have never treated a girl like this, I would have been pissed she didn't tell me to stop and would have shut her down, but this is so much fun, Anna thought to herself.

"Wow, Mommy's a whore," Anna said, nodding her head and digesting the words making Meg giggle.

"You're not, Mommy," Meg said, smiling at

Anna and melting her heart.

"No?" Anna said, opening her arms and having Meg cuddle into her.

"No. You're a predatory slut sure, but not a whore," Meg giggled, Anna looking at her in shock.

"Do you really think so? That is the nicest compliment anyone has ever given me!" Anna joked.

"Yeah, but I like it. Coz, you make me feel all protected and safe," Meg said, snuggling into Anna.

"I'm glad I make you feel safe even though I pushed you too far tonight," Anna said, making the conversation return to a serious manner.

"I'll say something next time," Meg said, making Anna smile.

"I'd like that. And I will learn your limits the longer we keep this going," Anna said, causing Meg to sit up.

"I don't want this to end," she said, looking fearful.

"No darling, either do I. I just meant that the more time I spend with you and your gorgeous body, the more I will learn how what your limits are. Oh god no, I don't ever want to give you up are you kidding me!" Anna replied, making Meg relax back into her arms.

Chapter 8

Meg raced around the corner, knowing that she was late. She had organized to meet up with a friend, after days of ignoring her messages.

"Hey, sorry I'm late," Meg said, panting slightly. She took her coat and scarf off, pulled out the chair, and sat down.

"Babe, where the hell have you been?!" Skyla questioned, looking at Meg expectantly.

"So. You'll never guess, you remember that seriously hot woman from the airport last Sunday? The one who wanted the sugar and then who I ended up sitting next to?" Meg said, jogging Skyla's memory.

"Yeah, the one who was a bit older, with the eyes," Skyla said, remembering how piercing Anna's green eyes were.

"Yep. Well, after I got all my shit and walked away from you guys, I took out the business card she gave me and called her. And I've been staying at hers ever since," Meg said, looking over the menu as she waited for Skyla to process the information.

"Hold up. So you meet someone on a plane, and then they put you up? Damn, the sex you must be giving her must be amazing," Skyla said, raising her eyebrows and shaking her head.

"It's not even like that. She is a. She gets me. I guess we are together actually," Meg said, realizing for the first time that she was potentially in a relationship.

"I like, don't mean to burst this happy bubble you've found yourself in, but like, what does she get out of having you there in her house?" Skyla seriously asked, putting her menu down and looking at Meg in the eye. This was not how Meg thought the lunch date would go at all.

"I can't get into it. But we give each other what the other person wants and needs. You wouldn't understand," Meg said before ordering a sandwich.

"No, what I understand is that you got with this woman, probably know next to nothing about her and haven't spoken to any of your friends in like, four days," Skyla said, folding her arms across her chest.

"I'm sorry you feel that way," Meg muttered to herself and shook her head.

"You know, I thought you'd be happy for me. Alex kicked me out, remember, I had nowhere to go and Anna," Meg said, getting cut off.

"Anna, what? Scooped you up off the street like you were some puppy in need of saving. Do you expect me to believe that?" Skyla said, raising her voice and frowning at Meg.

"You know what? I don't care what you fucking believe. She was there for me when no one else was, I was prepared to put all the aside and try to start fresh," Meg said, raising her voice to match Skyla's.

"We told you that you could crash with any one of us," Skyla defensively said.

"Yeah. And I am so grateful I didn't take up

the offer you backstabbing, bunch of bitches who sided with that fucking slut. I saw the photos, Skyla. I know all about the party on Friday night. How all of you went around to Alex's place and hung out all together like it was no big fucking deal," Meg said, slamming her hand down on the table. She hadn't sworn in over a week, and she had to admit, it felt damn good.

"Whatever. This was a mistake coming here. I hope you and your old lady have a great time together," Skyla said, getting up just as Meg's sandwich was put down in front of her.

"Yeah, I'm going to need this to go," Meg said to the waitress, getting up to put her coat and scarf back on before heading to the counter to pay.

Meg walked to the park, trying to block out the words Skyla had used.

She's just jealous. They are all jealous. Anna is awesome who cares about how we met. Meg thought to herself as she found an empty park bench and took out her sandwich.

She doesn't understand. None of them would. It's impossible to find a Mommy. Let alone one who is super rich, super beautiful, and super amazing in bed and as a Mommy. And we have things in common. We both like movies, and we both think that bourbon is better than Scotch, Meg thought, watching as the people passed her. She continued to eat her sandwich, never checking the time until she got a phone call, her phone vibrating in her pocket.

"Hey baby girl, where are you?" Anna said down the phone. Meg smiled as she heard the concern in Anna's voice.

"Well, I'm sitting in a park, eating my sandwich that I got to go because all my friends are crap, and I hate them all," Meg said, feeling sorry for herself.

"Oh. Do you want some company? It's getting dark. Are you somewhere safe?" Anna asked. Meg turned around to see that the park was darker than she had registered it being, the park lights having come on long ago.

"Um, I'm just in the park, by the water on the side closest to our, your place," Meg said.

"Baby, it's your place too. Ok. Can Mommy come down and sit with you?" Anna said. She had planned a night of pillow fort making but figured that Meg would need a different kind of loving tonight.

"Yeah, I'd like that," Meg said as she sniffed back a tear.

See? Anna is perfect. Meg thought as she hung up and waited for Anna to join her.

"There you are," Anna said, jogging up to Meg.

"Were you out for a run?" Meg asked as Anna came to sit next to her.

"No. I just thought it would be quicker to run here than to walk," Anna said, wrapping an arm around Meg.

"So, talk to me," Anna said, taking out her Air Pods and putting them in her jogging jacket.

"So I met up with Skyla, and she pretty

much just told me that it was weird that we only just met and moved in together like we were going too fast or something. She made it sound as though there was something suspicious about you or whatever," Meg said. She was annoyed that she had let Skyla get to her, as far as Meg was concerned she didn't have any friends anymore. They had all, for some reason, taken Alex's side. The various messages saying that she had been a shit girlfriend, that at least he was happy now and that she should try and just let it go so they could all hang out like old times was proof enough for her that those girls were never her friends.

"How do you feel about it all? I know it's a bit strange that we clicked right away, and it was fortunate for me, at least that you needed a place to stay. Do you think I crept on you too hard? Do you want me to help you get set up in your apartment?" Anna said. Hearing herself made her stomach churn.

Why am I suggesting any of this? I don't want to lose her. She thought to herself, sweeping the hair out of Meg's eyes.

"No. I don't want any of that. I just, I don't know. It just sucks that I lost all my friends," Meg said, bringing her knees up to her chest and holding onto them tightly.

"Can I offer a different perspective?" Anna asked, turning her body to face Meg and resting her arm on the back of the bench. Anna loved that her breasts pushed into Meg's arm, knowing that Meg would love it too and smiling when she put her legs down to snuggle into Anna.

"Sure," Meg softly said, holding onto Anna. Anna kissed the top of Meg's head, loving the sweet smell of her perfume.

"Maybe they weren't meant to be your friends forever. Maybe they were just friends until you found something more aligned with who you are and where you want to take your life?" Anna said, causing Meg to look up at her.

"But it hurts," Meg said, her whiny voice making Anna smile.

"Oh, I know it does, baby girl. I know it

does," Anna said, rocking Meg gently in her arms as she remembered the countless people she had lost along the way. People who disguised themselves as friends only to let her down. Anna took a deep breath before kissing Meg on the cheek.

"Come on. Come home with me and let me look after you tonight," Anna said, holding out her hand to Meg.

"Why do you even like me so much?" Meg said as she got up and took Anna's hand, remembering the question Skyla had posed to her. Anna stopped walking and turned Meg by the shoulders to look at her. Meg knew that she was either in serious trouble for asking. Either that or that Anna was about to talk about something serious by the look in her eye. Either way, Meg knew that Anna was deciding on how serious she was about to be.

"You give my heart a reason to feel. Before I met you, sure I had my fun, but I never felt that my heart truly felt. You changed that. You give me an outlet to be soft, kind, loving, and gentle instead of overly dominating and viewing everything as a hunt. You bring out the best in me," Anna said, tears forming in her eyes. Meg gasped, surprised that Anna was being so forthcoming and stood frozen, processing the words.

"My walls just crumbled down when I met you," Anna said, wiping her tears away and smiling at Meg before retaking her hand and beginning to walk out of the park.

"You should see the way the other people at the office scurry out of my way, as though I will open my mouth and breathe fire on them. They call me the dragon lady. But knowing that I have the sweetest baby girl to come home to, I can feel myself transition in the car drive home, and by the time I am opening up that front door, I know who I want to be," Anna explained leading Meg out onto the street. Meg turned her head, surprised they were going the wrong way home.

"Um, Mommy?" Meg questioned, Anna, continuing to walk, her grip on Meg's hand tightening.

"I think we need to get you some new friends, and I know just the place," Anna said, smiling down at Meg. Anna loosened her grip, feeling Meg struggling to break free.

"So all that stuff you just said, that's how you feel about me?" Meg asked, making Anna laugh as she pushed the door open to a dark and rough looking pub.

"Yeah. I hope you can handle Mommy getting a little bit emotional now and then," Anna laughed as she felt Meg wrap her arms around her.

"I liked it," Meg replied, before turning her head toward the open door and looked inside the pub. It looked like a standard pub. Meg thought that Anna had taken her here for a drink, and although she wasn't one to make friends at a pub, she shrugged her shoulders and walked in.

"Get two of whatever you want, honey. I don't care what I drink," Anna said, handing Meg her card before disappearing. Meg smiled. She loved it when Anna gave her her credit card. She ordered two long island iced teas and waited for Anna at the bar. As she looked out over the crowd, she started to see it and smirked. This was no ordinary night at an ordinary bar, as Meg had first thought. It was some sort of kink enthusiast gathering. It was the subtle details that gave it away, a leather collar on a girl with a gorgeous pink cocktail dress who had the men watching her as she danced mesmerized. The way a man was standing next to a woman, as he waited patiently, looking at the ground while she spoke to a friend. Another woman was lazily petting the head of a man sitting on a bench as she stood next to him. As Meg's eyes slowly scanned the crowd, she saw Anna walking across the dance floor and join a group of women talking in a circle.

I guess they are the Mommies. Meg thought as she saw the cuddly figures of the women. Meg could also tell by the energy they gave off. It wasn't the stern or predatory gaze that the other groups of people had. It was soft, gentle, but with just enough control that you knew not to mess with them. Anna caught Meg's eye and winked at her before excusing herself and walking in Meg's direction.

"Baby girl, I want you to meet some of my friends," Anna said, taking her drink in one hand and Meg's wrist in the other.

"Ok," Meg replied, Anna, stopping immediately.

"Oh, I didn't think you would be shy about it. Do you get shy when you meet new people, baby girl?" Anna said, enjoying learning this about Meg, who nodded her head.

"Well. You don't need to be. There isn't any protocol here tonight, that's why there are so many people from so many kinks. It's just a night where everybody can make it as kinky or vanilla as they like. So just be yourself, and if your little self comes out, then Mommy will look after you, alright?" Anna said lovingly. Meg was wildly aware that the group of women were looking at her and bit her lip before nodding her head and walking behind Anna as they approached the group.

"This is Meg. This is Rachael, Belinda, and Carmen," Anna said, introducing the women. Meg politely smiled, sipped her drink as she listened to their conversation. Anna had known these women for a long time as Meg heard them sharing stories from years ago.

As the night grew on, Meg began to get increasingly drunk, enjoying the feeling of finally being able to relax.

"I've had the world's craziest week," Meg said to a guy she had just met.

"Really? Tell me about it?" He asked. Meg just laughed and shook her head.

"I don't even know your name!" She said, causing Anna to turn around, watching the two talk.

"It looks like you little one and mine are getting along," Anna said to Carmen, who turned to look as well.

"That's sweet. It's what you wanted, wasn't it? That Meg finds some people that she has something in common with," Carmen said as they turned back around to finish their conversation.

"I'm Garret. I'm with Carmen," Garret said, pointing to where she was sitting.

"Like with with, or like, with, you know," Meg said, beginning to blush.

"Like, yeah, she's my Mommy," Garret said. He rarely said that out loud, but hearing himself say it made him smile.

"So, now you know my name, what's yours," Garret asked, ordering another beer.

"Meg," Meg replied, sipping her drink.

"So my week went like this. I find out my boyfriend is cheating on me with my ex-best friend, I meet Anna in a café, and then we sit next to each other on the plane ride home and then she gives me her business card and says to call her if I need her," Meg said, pausing as Anna and Carmen came over.

"And then we lived happily ever after," Anna said, kissing Meg on the mouth.

"Dude, do you know how lucky you are?" Garret said, coping a whack on the back of his head.

"I know I'm lucky," Garret said, rubbing his head.

"No, my rude little boy is right," Carmen said, eyeing Garret.

"Anna has turned down many little offers, you must be something pretty special," Carmen said, smiling at Meg. Meg wrapped her arm around Anna's waist and hugged her tight. In her drunken state, she was worried that if she let Anna go, somebody else might come and take her heart.

"Ready to go?" Anna asked, paying the tab off and putting her card in her purse. Just as she saw a group of women in latex dresses, walk in catching Meg's eye.

"I'd say it was time for us to go too," Carmen said, laughing at the way Garret and Meg looked at the women.

"Where are they going?" Meg whispered to Anna as the women walked up the stairs of the outdoor area.

"Someplace where you are not. It's way

past your bedtime," Anna said, making Meg giggle.

"Mommy," Meg cooed, trying her hardest to change Anna's mind.

"Don't Mommy me, young lady," Anna said in the tone that made Meg squash any desire to continue to test her. Anna held out her hand and smiled as Meg jumped down from her stool and walked out her with, onto to the street.

"We will have to have a play date sometime," Carmen said, holding Garret's hand. Garret was bigger than Carmen, and anybody looking at the pair would think their dynamic was the other way around, especially when Garret shoved a guy out of the way when he bumped into them.

"Watch it, bro," Garret said, looking at the guy with a challenging stare. Garret had big muscles from years as a personal trainer, and the other guy thought it better not to pick a fight with him.

"Oh, my sweet baby boy," Carmen said, kissing Garret's chest before turning back to Anna and Meg.

"Yeah, well. What about Tomorrow afternoon? That way, if the babies get too tired, you can stay over?" Anna offered, Carmen agreeing and the two women kissed each other on the cheek before they parted ways for the night.

"Mommy," Meg softly said as she walked alongside Anna, who was walking very fast to get out of the cold.

"Yes?" Anna said, looking straight ahead.

"What if I'm like, what if he is more of a real baby, and I'm like, a fake or something?" Meg nervously said. Anna wished it wasn't so cold so she could stop walking and give Meg the undivided attention the question begged.

"Baby girl. There is no right or wrong way to be little. I know littles who live the headspace 24/7, and I know littles who only have a stuffie. It's the same with Mommies too. Everybody is different, and even if Garret and Carmen do things differently to us, it doesn't make them right or wrong. It doesn't make us right or wrong, it just means that what we do is right for us and what they do is right for them," Anna explained, grateful to be inside the elevator of the apartment.

"That makes sense," Meg softly said, thinking about the words Anna said.

"And anyway, you are such a baby, what are you even worried about," Anna teased opening the door to the apartment and looking over the mess of toys and bottles Meg had failed to tidy up before she had left the house.

"You know. Mommy did tell you not to leave the house looking like a mess, did I?" Anna said, the warning in her tone mixed with the alcohol running through Meg's veins, making her unsure if she was going to hate or love what came next.

"Yes, but I thought that I'd be home before you got home. I thought I had time to tidy it up," Meg said, impressed at the case she was putting forward.

"And yet, despite what you think, Mommy still sees a mess," Anna whispered, stripping Meg of any confidence she had that she would get out of this situation without her ass being spanked. Anna walked to the bathroom, stripped her clothes off, and put on her high heels, sighing in content as she ran her hands over her body. She walked to her bedroom, took out her flogger before walking back to the living room, where she saw Meg trying to tidy up.

"Oh, nice try," Anna laughed, enjoying the frenzied pace Meg was going.

"Get your ass over here," Anna said, her angry Mommy tone making Meg stop dead in her tracks. Anna sat down on the lounge, picked up Meg's paci, and patter her thighs, waiting for Meg to obey her.

"You know, little girls who break Mommy's rules make me mad," Anna said, pushing the pacifier into Meg's mouth and holding her arm around Meg's neck and her hand firmly placed on Meg's mouth.

"So this is what I'm going to do. Your little ass is going to be flogged until it is so red, that every time you think about breaking one of Mommy's rules, you remember how much this hurt and you do everything, and I mean everything in your power not to break my rules again," Anna said, bringing her flogger down on Meg's ass and getting turned on immediately by the squeal it elicited from Meg.

"That's what I want to hear little girl," Anna said, flogging Meg three more times before she stopped and rubbed her ass cheeks.

"Let Mommy see how red you are," Anna said, pulling down Meg's pants, smiling as she saw her pussy glisten.

"Does this turn the baby on?" Anna whispered as she slid her finger up and down Meg's wet slit making her moan against Anna's hand. Arching her back, Meg ached to be touched, making Anna laugh.

"Do you think, after you broke Mommy's rule, I am going to reward you by touching your pussy?" Anna said, pushing two fingers into Meg suddenly, making her moan.

"Is that what you want? To be fucked by Mommy," Anna said, pounding Meg hard and fast before pulling out of her just as she felt herself reach the edge of her orgasm. Groaning in frustration, Meg bucked her hips aggressively, stopping once she felt the flogger strike her ass.

"Don't get greedy," Anna said, waiting for the sting she knew Meg would have just felt subside slightly before flogging her again.

"So red, so wet, I bet you would do almost anything to stop this and have your pussy fucked instead," Anna said, kissing the top of Meg's head before flogging her again. Anna put her whip down, grabbed Meg by the hair, and pulled her into a room she hadn't been into.

"You are so lucky to be coming in here," Anna said, unlocking the door. Meg's eyes grew wide as she saw the space. Taking out her paci, Meg looked around the room.

"Mommy?" Meg questioned, seeing the BDSM dungeon.

"I have a few kinks," Anna said, pushing

Meg down on the bed. She cuffed Meg's wrists and ankles to the bedposts before standing back and looking at Meg.

"Such a beautiful little body," Anna cooed, taking a clit suction vibrator out of her cupboard. She replaced the paci with the dildo end of the toy, enjoying how Meg began sucking it straight away.

"Such a good girl," Anna cooed, watching her get it wet before taking it out and sliding it into Meg's pussy.

"You know how to take it, don't you little one," Anna teased, taking a pair of latex panties and gently dressing Meg, pulling them on over the toy, which was now also sucking on her clit. Anna loved hearing the moans coming from Meg, but worried that the neighbors might make a noise complaint, she took a gag and placed it in her mouth.

"Mommy is going to keep you like that while I finish tidying up the mess I shouldn't have had to see," Anna said, tenderly touching Meg's body and kissing her down her body before she shut the door leaving Meg in darkness as she was forced to orgasm over and over.

Anna knew that after ten minutes, Meg would be ready to fuck her way to freedom. She loved that about the girl, she sure knew how to use her body. Coming back into the room, Meg was blinded by the hallway light, closing her eyes as she felt another orgasm pulse through her body.

"What pretty little sounds," Anna cooed, coming to sit down next to Meg.

"Mommy doesn't think you've learned your lesson, I can see how hard your nipples are through your sweater," Anna teased, running her hands over Meg's breasts.

"No bra today? You were feeling little," Anna said, reaching under, delighted to find Meg's exposed breasts. Anna uncuffed Meg's ankles and wrists, happy that the girl stayed still once she was freed.

"Mommy has a special surprise for you. I must have known when I started taking the pills that I would have a little girl who needed me soon enough," Anna said, taking her top and bra off. She played with her breasts, loving how Meg moaned as she watched.

"Yeah, I know you love them," Anna said, wondering how she got so lucky to have this gorgeous creature so obsessed with her.

"Let me taking this off," Anna said, reaching for the gag, pulling Meg onto her lap and pushing her nipple into Meg's mouth, holding her head firmly in place. Anna smiled down at Meg as Meg's eyes grew wide, not expecting to taste milk.

"Now you won't have to drink from a bottle, you can drink from Mommy just the way you need little girl," Anna said, stroking Meg's face. Meg closed her eyes as another orgasm hit her, suckling hard as her body went rigid then fell limp in Anna's arms.

"I know baby girl," Anna said as Meg began to shake her head, signaling to Anna that her limit was wildly close to being reached. Anna loved that Meg held her breast with both hands as she rolled down the latex panties and pulled the toy from her cunt, leaving both of them in a pile on the bed.

"Mommy's pretty girl," Anna cooed, surprised at how connected she felt to Meg, who looked up at her with her big eyes as she suckled.

Chapter 9

"Is this ok?" Meg said, running down the hallway for the third time to show Anna her latest outfit choice.

"If I had known a simple get together would have turned into this, I wouldn't have suggested it," Anna said, the amusement showing on her face.

"Mommy, I don't have time for this, they are going to be here in like ten minutes," Meg half squealed as she twirled for Anna. This time she had opted for her combat boots, black denim mini skirt, and the fluffy pink sweater that Anna had first noticed her in.

"Well, if you want Mommy's clit to be hard for the whole time, then yes, this is the outfit for you," Anna said, grabbing the hem of Meg's skirt and pulling her closer to her before touching her through her panties.

"Mommy," Meg whined, feeling Anna pull

her panties to the slide and tease her pussy lips open just as a knock came from the door.

"Saved by the bell," Anna whispered in Meg's ear, getting up and walking toward the door.

"Guess that's what you are wearing," Anna said, turning around and winking at Meg before opening the door.

"Carmen," Anna greeted, opening her arms and warmly embracing the woman. Meg peaked her head around the corner.

"Oh, sweetie, Garret will be here shortly. He is just training a client at the moment," Carmen said, smiling warmly at Meg, who gave her a sad sideward smile before going out to the patio.

"So, drink?" Anna said, leading Carmen into the living room. Anna smiled at Meg, who sat on her phone in the afternoon winter sun.

"She's a sweet girl," Carmen said, eyeing Meg.

"Don't even think about it. She's all mine," Anna said, making Carmen laugh.

"Anyway, I'd of thought you'd have your

hands full with Garret, quite literally," Anna said, drawing subtle attention to the monster she knew Garret was packing.

"Yeah. It's been a bit weird between us lately. I'm not sure what to think of it. Everything just seems so predictable," Carmen said, sipping the cocktail Anna had made them both moments before she had arrived.

"I get that. I worry about that with Meg, especially since it was going at 100 miles per hour, the minute we got together. I was worried for a moment that it would be a fast-burning candle and that it would be over as quickly as it started," Anna said, admiring how Meg's blonde hair was swept up in the wind.

"He has taken on more clients, working later than he ever has. He says it's because he wants to grow his reputation and client base, but it feels as though he is almost trying to get away from me," Carmen said, sighing.

"I don't know, maybe I'm being paranoid or something," Carmen quickly added.

"I don't think you are. These feelings often have some truth to them," Anna said, making Carmen laugh.

"That doesn't make me feel any better," she said, Anna just smirking.

"If you want to be soothed, let me get you a pacifier to suck on, you know me better than to bullshit with you," Anna teased making Carmen roll her eyes.

"You know. I know why Meg is so smitten with you, you are the only woman I know who can make another Mommy feel like a little with one sentence. That is some damn fine mind work you are wielding," Carmen said, getting up to get another drink.

"So, what do you think you should do?" Anna said, taking a strawberry from the bowl in front of her.

"I don't know any suggestions?" Carmen said, making Anna laugh.

"You know, you just don't want to do it," Anna said, looking up as she saw Meg walk through the glass doors. Patting her lap, Anna uncrossed her legs and smiled as Meg settled against her.

"You need to show him who is boss. Who he belongs to and what happens when he breaks a rule. It sounds to me like he has broken quite a few, not communicating his needs with you, withholding his truth, and the biggest one, wasting your goddamn time trying to figure out what his bratty, moody ass is up too," Anna said making Meg smirk.

"Mommy, you swore," Meg whispered, making Anna chuckle.

"Mommy can do what she wants, you on the other hand," Anna said, squeezing Meg tight.

"Withholding his truth?" Meg asked, turning her head to face Anna.

"We aren't at that stage yet, baby girl, it'll come but not yet," Anna said, reassuring Meg. She knew that Meg would be thinking about that for the next few hours, and Anna stroked her thigh lovingly, not wanting Meg to let her mind run off with thoughts that she wasn't doing something right.

"You're welcome to use the dungeon if you need to," Anna offered just as a knock came from the door.

"I might take you up on that offer," Carmen said, getting up to open the door.

"Hey, sorry I'm late," Garret said, walking into the room and passed Carmen. Anna wasn't impressed at the lack of attention he gave Carmen. She was even less impressed by how his eyes lit up when he saw Meg. As Garret walked over to greet Meg, Anna shifted her on her lap and held a foot out, stopping him.

"Go and kiss your Mama hello," Anna said, Garret's face falling before he turned and walked back to Carmen. Carmen and Anna had discussed how this afternoon would go, and as Anna looked at Meg's wide eyes, she knew that it was going to be fun.

"What is happening?" Meg whispered in Anna's ear as her head rested on her shoulder.

"This is what happens to naughty boys who don't listen to their Mommy's. It takes a village, after all, little girl," Anna replied, stroking Meg's back.

"But I've been good?" Meg asked, making Anna's heart swell.

"Yes, baby girl, you've been perfect," Anna replied, kissing her on the tip of her nose before turning her head to watch Garret and Carmen. Garret had leaned forward to kiss Carmen on the lips, wincing as she slapped his cheek.

"Try again," Carmen said, her frustration evident in her voice. Garret shifted from foot to foot, not wanting to get in wrong again and slowly bent his knees until he knelt before Carmen, who had her hand on her hips.

"Lower," Carmen instructed when Garret tried to kiss her pussy. He bit his bottom lip and placed his hands on the floor as he looked up from Carmen's feet, she raised eyebrow telling him that he finally got it right.

"Don't make wait any longer," Carmen said,

watching as Garret blushed and began to kiss her boot as her other foot rested on his back, keeping him in place.

"I didn't think littles would like that," Meg softly said, only realizing that she was sucking her thumb when she tried to speak. Making Anna hum happily.

"As I said, it depends on the people involved. Garret is a strong-willed little. He can be the best little boy in the world, but my god does he have a stubborn streak, and this has been the best way he has learned to correct that bratty behavior. There's always something you can learn about yourself, like how you learned you don't like being called a whore. He learned through experience that to get back to being good. He needs a strong hand," Anna explained as she watched Carmen switch boots.

"You know," Anna loudly said, winking at Meg and patting her bottom to get her to stand up before standing up herself and walking over to Carmen and Garret.

"I don't think he deserves these nice clothes you buy him," Anna said, reaching down and roughly stripping him. Meg was surprised at Anna's strength. She never used such a firm hand on her. Carmen crossed her arms and enjoyed watching Anna tear at Garret's clothes until he was naked.

"There. If you are going to act like a naughty little boy, that's exactly how you are going to be treated," Anna said, kicking his clothes away. Garret stood standing in front of the women naked, covering himself, which just made Carmen laugh.

"Oh, don't hide it away when you were so happy swinging it around to try and impress little Meg," Carmen said, making him blush.

"That's what I thought," Carmen said, looking over at Meg, who shifted uncomfortably.

"I didn't mean to make him think he had a chance," Meg said, Anna, smiling in amusement.

"Oh no, sweetie, that's just it. This naughty boy thinks he has a chance with everyone, don't you? Have you forgotten who looks after you? Who buys your clothes, who soothes you when you get nightmares and wipes your tears away when you feel scared?" Carmen said, turning back to face Garret.

"I. I'm sorry, Mommy," Garret said, feeling himself being pulled into little space. He sighed, finally feeling relief and dropped his head.

"There you are. Mommy's good little boy. Did all those weights and protein shakes and skinny girls in tight leggings make you forget that Mommy is the one who looks after you?" Carmen said, going softer on him than Anna would have.

"Yes, Mommy. I just," Garret said, blushing and looking up.

"I just thought I was the man and thought that I didn't need you to be my Mommy anymore. But I was wrong," Garret said, beginning to cry. Anna raised her eyebrow and headed back to Meg, who was standing as still as a statue.

"Come on, little one," Anna softly said, taking the bowl of strawberries in one hand and

Meg's hand in the other and led her outside to the patio and curled up with her on the day bed.

"What just happened?" Meg asked before Anna put a strawberry in her mouth.

"Like, if he wanted to break up with her, why didn't he just say?" Meg said as she gulped the fruit so she could finish her question.

"He never wanted to leave her. It's kind of like. Sometimes when a little stays out of little space for a long time, they can start to be bratty because they miss being a little. They miss the relief of it. But work can get in the way, life can just happen so fast, and before you know it, you're a brat to try and push the other person into giving you attention because you don't know how to ask for what you want. It can happen when two people have been together for a long time. Then they start fighting and then sometimes if they don't fix it they break up. But this was easily fixed," Anna explained as Meg listened attentively.

"So, he never wanted to leave her? He just wanted to be little but couldn't get into little space?" Meg asked, clarifying what Anna just described.

"In this situation, yeah. But you need to understand, they have been together for ten years, they know each other well. They have the understanding that I can be a part of their dynamic to a certain degree. I know it seemed like it was all spontaneous, but it was all planned last night when you were asleep. I'm sorry I didn't tell you, do you think that I should have?" Anna asked, suddenly realizing that she really should have told Meg a few key points about the afternoon.

"Um, yes!" Meg exclaimed, laughing.

"Hello? I just saw a stranger naked," Meg continued making Anna laugh.

"Yeah, ok, my bad, can you forgive Mommy?" Anna said, making Meg laugh.

"I think you need to be punished, Mommy," Meg teased, getting tickled by Anna.

"Don't make it hurt too much, I have an important meeting on Monday," Anna laughed.

"Oh, no, I'm not going to hurt you there, we

are going to go shopping," Meg giggled, Anna, raising an eyebrow.

"What, you told me that half the fun of punishment is the enjoyment it brings both people, and we both like to shop, so," Meg said as Anna began to nod in agreeance.

"Well, I guess we are going shopping," Anna said, watching as the sunset over the city.

Chapter 10

Carmen and Garret came out to the patio an hour later, just as Meg and Anna were about to come inside.

"Thanks, Miss Anna," Garret said, smiling at her bashfully.

"My pleasure, baby boy," Anna replied, reaching out and stroking Garret's face.

"Would you like to stay for dinner?" Anna asked Carmen, who smiled at her gratefully.

"Not tonight, I need to get my little prince home and tucked into bed. It's been a big day for him," Carmen said, hugging Anna affectionately before waving goodbye to Meg and leaving the apartment.

"I never want to be that naughty," Meg said once the door was shut.

"Oh, you'll be plenty naughty, you don't need to worry about that," Anna teased, grabbing at Meg's hem of her skirt.

"Now, where was I," Anna questioned playfully.

"Oh, yes," she continued, feeling Meg's wet slit.

"Mommy," Meg said, pushing Anna's hands away and shaking her head.

"Ok, dinner, bathies, and bedtime cuddles?" Anna said, making Meg smile.
Anna tidied the kitchen, placing the empty bowl and glasses in the dishwasher before taking two pieces of salmon out of the freezer.

"Fish and chips work for you?" Anna called from the kitchen. Meg had run to the nursery and brought out the train set and was putting the tracks together.

"That sounds yummy, Mommy," Meg replied happily. She knew that it wouldn't be the standard fish and chips. Nothing about Anna was standard as she looked into the kitchen and saw the potatoes being cut and rosemary being sprinkled over the top, she knew that this dinner wouldn't be standard either.

Meg hadn't realized she had fallen asleep until Anna was gently rocking her awake.

"Hey there, little one," Anna said, smiling down on Meg. Meg scrunched her face up and rolled over, rolling onto one of her trains and was suddenly very awake.

"Ouch," she said, turning back to face Anna.

"What time is it?" Meg asked as she rubbed her hand.

"11:00. I wanted to let you sleep, but I need to get you ready for bed, and you weren't waking up," Anna replied, taking Meg's wrist in her hand and standing her up.

"Mommy," Meg said as Anna wrapped her arm around the girl and pulled her smaller body into hers.

"Gosh, you just fit perfectly in my arms," Anna said, stroking Meg's hair out of the way. Anna kissed Meg's forehead before walking with her down the hallway and into the bathroom.

"Just a quick shower tonight, little one," Anna said as she turned the water on before walking out the other side of the open shower and taking her clothes off.

"Mommy, can you help?" Meg said as she wearily pulled on her clothes, making Anna smirk.

"What's the magic word?" Anna questioned as she stood in front of Meg, who had somehow trapped herself in her sweater.

"Please, Mommy," Meg said, feeling Anna's hands on her body, giving her goosebumps as she helped her.

"There," Anna said, taking off Meg's skirt, panties, and bra. Meg had long since taken off her combat boots and socks, and she let Anna tie her hair up as not to get it wet.

"Here, clean your teeth in the shower as well. It'll get you into bed quicker," Anna said, passing Meg her toothbrush.

"Ok," Meg wearily said, wishing the Anna would brush her teeth for her, holding out the toothbrush to her and hoping that Anna would read her mind.

"Does the baby need Mommy to brush her teethies?" Anna said, rinsing Meg's body of any soap.

"Yes, please, Mommy," Meg said as she closed her eyes and melted into Anna's warm embrace as she brushed her teeth.

"Such a sweet little girl," Anna said, letting Meg spit the toothpaste out before turning off the shower.

"Mommy has put the towels on the heating racks baby girl, yours is the blue one," Anna said, pointing to the towel. Meg nodded and went over, taking it down and wrapping herself in it but drying her feet first, making Anna laugh.

"You sure do hate your feet or fingers not being dry, don't you," she said as Meg nodded.

"And other things," Meg said, causing Anna to tilt her head in curiosity.

"Like?" Anna asked as she wrapped her towel around her hips and walked to her bedroom, Meg, in tow.

"Like, I like my diaper dry too," Meg said, referring to a conversation she and Anna had had earlier in the week.

"I see. Still trying to tell Mommy that you're not going to wet your diaper?" Anna said, trying to hide her amusement.

"Yes," Meg said, nodding her head and looking very serious.

"Well, let's just put this on you, just in case," Anna said, taking a thick diaper and putting it on Meg, who huffed and looked away, crossing her arms over her chest.

"Oh, pouty little thing. Does Mommy have to correct that?" Anna said, grabbing hold of Meg's thighs and squeezing.

"No, Mommy," Meg gasped, remembering how long and tiresome Anna made her punishments.

"Good," Anna quickly said, getting up and going to the cupboard, taking out Meg's jammies.

"You are going to look so sweet in these. I picked them up on the way home this week but was waiting until we had some time so I could enjoy them," Anna said, showing Meg the crocodile print flannel pajamas. Meg smiled excitedly and reached for them.

"They have little Sven's on them, Mommy!" Meg exclaimed, melting Anna's heart.

"I know. I thought, who do I know who would like these? Do you know anyone?" Anna teased, pulling the pants over Meg's diaper and rolling them up until they were mid-calf.

"Me, Mommy," Meg squealed, making Anna laugh.

"You are so cute," Anna said, doing the buttons up on the front.

"If there was ever a little girl who could pull off crocodile jammies, it would be you," Anna said, looking at Meg's messy blonde hair, her sweet, ever so kissable lips and big innocent eyes.

"Come on, get under these covers and wait for Mommy to get ready," Anna said as she took both towels back into the bathroom. Meg waited with her thumb in her mouth, her eyelids growing heavy, and as Anna came back into the room, she sighed and smiled.

"Oh, baby girl," she softly said, turning the light off and walking out into the living room.

It was nearing midnight, but Anna wasn't interested in sleeping. The tension she felt dominating Garret at even the small level she had that day had kept her blood hot, even now. Taking her phone out, she called Carmen, who she knew would still be awake as well.

"Hey. How did it go when you got home?" Anna said as she made herself a tea.

"So good. We had a long talk, turned out he needed me to give him more rules, he didn't think he was serving me enough, even as a little," Carmen replied, as Anna went to sit by the window.

"Aww, he just wanted to serve his Mommy," Anna laughed.

"That's quite sweet," she added.

"Yeah. It was. He was like, I don't feel like I have to do anything like you don't need me,"

Carmen said, piquing Anna's interest.

"Wow, no wonder he was acting out," Anna said, as she saw Meg walking out to her. Anna reached out to Meg, frowning when she didn't come to her, shaking her head instead.

"Babe, I've got to go. I'm glad it all worked out for you guys," Anna said, hanging up the phone. Anna looked at Meg for a moment, her initial anger that she was ignored fading when she saw the emotional look on Meg's face.

"Mommy," Meg said in her soft, little voice, looking down at her diaper. Meg held onto Sven's tail and sucked her thumb.

"Oh, baby girl," Anna said, lovingly smiling as she learned what Meg was trying to tell her.

"It's ok, sweetie. Mommy can just clean you up and change you," Anna said, standing up and walking over to Meg, who burst into tears.

"But I didn't want to," Meg said, Anna, bending down slightly and wiping her tears away.

"Sometimes, when we are relaxed, these things happen. Come on," Anna said, taking Meg's hand and leading her back into the nursery. Anna directed her to the mat, took off her pajama bottoms, and took off the wet diaper. She wiped Meg clean and sprinkled fresh powder over her, making her giggle as it tickled her body.

"There's my happy little one," Anna said as she fastened a fresh diaper to Meg's waist before pulling on her jammie pants again.

"There. That wasn't so bad, was it?" Anna said, Meg's pursed lips telling her that maybe it was.

"Do you want to cuddle Mommy while you fall back asleep, honey?" Anna asked, already knowing the answer. Meg rubbed her eyes and nodded her head. Anna walked back to the living room to put her mug in the dishwasher as Meg crawled into bed.

"Come to Mommy," Anna said, pulling Meg into her and taking her thumb out of her mouth, smirking when Meg whined.

"Don't whine baby girl, Mommy only takes things away when I'm about to give you something better," Anna said, pushing her nipple pasts Meg's lips and settling her as she closed her eyes and started to suckle.

"Mommy's pretty girl," Anna cooed as she patted Meg's bottom as she fell back asleep in the arms of her loving Mommy.

Who is Tina Moore?

Tina Moore has enjoyed the lifestyle of a Mommy Domme for several years. She began secretly exploring kink and BDSM in her youth and found her love of being a strict Mommy Domme in early 2000. Tina Moore slowly became more comfortable and confident through making friends in the community and exploring the lifestyle and now openly celebrates being a Mommy Domme to her little.

Before becoming an author, Tina Moore worked in the finance sector, but it was through the encouragement of her current little that she took the leap and wrote her first MDLG book, Nancy's Little One.

From then on, Tina Moore continued to combine her experiences and desires, as well as the sweet and naughty things her baby girl does, to bring you tantalizing and salacious stories about both MDLG and DDLG relationships and the ABDL littles and middles who enjoy them.

Follow her on:
Author Page on Amazon
Instagram @tinamoore.kdp

www.ingramcontent.com/pod-product-compliance
Lightning Source LLC
Chambersburg PA
CBHW031023190726
48286CB00003BA/991